FANGS FOR FREAKS

Berkley titles by Serena Robar

BRACED TO BITE

FANGS FOR FREAKS

DATING FOR DEMONS

FANGS FOR FREAKS

SERENA ROBAR

BERKLEY BOOKS, NEW YORK

THE BERKLEY PUBLISHING GROUP
Published by the Penguin Group
Penguin Group (USA) Inc.
375 Hudson Street, New York, New York 10014, USA
Penguin Group (Canada), 90 Eglinton Avenue East, Suite 700, Toronto, Ontario M4P 2Y3, Canada
(a division of Pearson Penguin Canada Inc.)
Penguin Books Ltd., 80 Strand, London WC2R 0RL, England
Penguin Group Ireland, 25 St. Stephen's Green, Dublin 2, Ireland (a division of Penguin Books Ltd.)
Penguin Group (Australia), 250 Camberwell Road, Camberwell, Victoria 3124, Australia
(a division of Pearson Australia Group Pty. Ltd.)
Penguin Books India Pvt. Ltd., 11 Community Centre, Panchsheel Park, New Delhi—110 017, India
Penguin Group (NZ), 67 Apollo Drive, Rosedale, North Shore 0632, New Zealand
(a division of Pearson New Zealand Ltd.)
Penguin Books (South Africa) (Pty.) Ltd., 24 Sturdee Avenue, Rosebank, Johannesburg 2196,
South Africa

Penguin Books Ltd., Registered Offices: 80 Strand, London WC2R 0RL, England

This is a work of fiction. Names, characters, places, and incidents either are the product of the author's imagination or are used fictitiously, and any resemblance to actual persons, living or dead, business establishments, events, or locales is entirely coincidental. The publisher does not have any control over and does not assume any responsibility for author or third-party websites or their content.

PRINTING HISTORY
Berkley JAM trade paperback edition / November 2006
Berkley trade paperback edition / July 2010

Berkley trade paperback ISBN: 978-0-425-23765-6

The Library of Congress has cataloged the Berkley JAM trade paperback edition as follows:

Robar, Serena.
    Fangs4freaks / Serena Robar. — Berkley Jam trade paperback ed.
        p. cm.
    Summary: As Protector of the half-blood vampires, Colby is called into action when her sisters in the newly established Psi Phi sorority house start experiencing ugly, unexpected attacks, either from a member of the Vampire Tribunal, or from a spy.
    ISBN 0-425-21195-9
    [1. Vampires—Fiction. 2. Best friends—Fiction. 3. Friendship—Fiction. 4. Universities and colleges—Fiction. 5. Horror stories.] I. Title. II. Title: Fangs 4 freaks. III. Title: Fangs for freaks.
PZ7.R5312Fan 2006
[Fic]—dc22

                                                                            2006020547

PRINTED IN THE UNITED STATES OF AMERICA

10 9 8 7 6 5 4 3 2 1

*This book is dedicated to my husband, Jason,
without whose unflagging support I could not begin to pen
the stories in my heart. Or buy the shoes in my closet.*

Acknowledgments

There is always someone who comes along and makes a good book better.

Special thanks to Holly Henderson-Root at Trident Media Group, who acted as my second set of eyes; my Goddess Divine agent, Jenny Bent; and to my brilliant, hardworking editor, Cindy Hwang, who knew exactly what tweaks were needed to give *Fangs* more bite.

Hehe. Bite. Get it?

One

A body launched from the bushes, straight at me, before I had time to register who or what it was. The force of the impact alone was enough to knock the breath from my lungs—that is, if I breathed. Instead of crushing me, I rolled with his momentum and neatly turned over once, then used my feet to send him flying over my head, crashing into crates of recycling awaiting pickup on the sidewalk.

Doing a quick flip from my back onto my feet, I, Colby Blanchard, moved toward my would-be assailant without trepidation.

"Are you okay, Cyrus?" I questioned, looking for signs of injury as he lay sprawled among the old newspapers and empty soda cans.

"Mmmph," came his muffled reply as he disentangled

himself from the bins, ". . . finish me?" He stood and I was relieved to find him relatively unharmed.

"What did you say?" I asked, a bit dubious of his reply. His left pant leg was ripped at the knee and I could see the scraped skin starting to bleed.

The scent of fresh blood filled my senses and I had to take a step back. A familiar ache in the roof of my mouth and loud rumbling from my stomach reminded me I hadn't fed last night. My treacherous hand involuntarily reached for the pocket housing specialized orthodontic headgear embedded with stainless-steel fangs. What? Just because I'm fang-handicapped doesn't make me a freak or anything. I can still get the job done, ya know. Just not right now. Now it was a battle of wills, between my true self and the inner demon who demanded to feed.

I took a Zen moment and subdued my hunger. It was so not getting the upper hand here. The first rule of thumb was no feeding on friends, and I wasn't about to break it because I was feeling a bit peckish.

"I said, why didn't you finish me off? You stood there like some clueless victim waiting for me to find a weapon to take you down."

"Uh, I knew it was you?" It was an obvious answer, but Cyrus was always all business.

For the last eight months, Cyrus spent two hours a day teaching me how to fight and protect myself. I met him on a routine visit to see Great-Aunt Chloe at her condo in Providence Point. Her neighbor, Bits Walker, was bragging about her grandson, a self-defense instructor and former special operative in the military. Like anything Bits said, I took it with a grain of salt. After all, she'd been married four times but on last count, she mentioned seven husbands. I wondered if perhaps she wasn't all there.

But one day, there was Cyrus, holding Bits's yarn as she knitted and listening attentively to her stories. He was smaller than I imagined, with craggy skin and a wicked-looking scar across his chin to his left ear, which appeared to be partially missing. He was wiry and muscular. I doubted he had an ounce of fat on his frame.

My thoughts were interrupted by Cyrus digging around the refuse. "What are you looking for?" I asked skeptically. Cyrus was, well, let's just say he and his grandmother were very alike in the sanity department.

"Aha!" he shouted triumphantly, brandishing what appeared to be a sharpened piece of wood.

"You had a stake?!" I gasped incredulously.

"It's like I'm having a conversation with Jell-o," he muttered to himself. "Of course. Did you think I was going to continue attacking you with just my bare hands? You are far too advanced for those tactics. At least, I thought you were. I thought you had achieved the black zone."

Oh crap, not the zones again.

When he first started training me, I was in the white zone, which meant I was completely oblivious to my surroundings. Then came the blue zone or was it the green? I could never keep them straight. Anyway, I quickly raced up the zones to the black zone, which meant I was in ninja-like awareness all the time. Personally, I liked being in the white zone, but when you're the most unpopular half-blood Undead in the neighborhood, you couldn't afford to be in the white zone anymore.

Ever since I was attacked and turned into a vampire—oh, excuse me, that would be *half-blood* vampire—I'd become persona non grata in the Undead community. I think I might have been able to live out my days in relative peace and solitude if I hadn't petitioned for half-blood rights and emancipated an entire species. That move made me a little less than popular with the full-blood population. Well, *excuse me* for fighting injustice.

I did such a good job at freeing my people, I was elevated to being their Protector, which I am sure was the Tribunal's way of getting rid of all of us. I imagine they were still kicking themselves that not only was I Undead and around, I was becoming a pretty kick-ass Protector in the process.

Today was the day I would meet the rest of my half-blood family. Yep, we were going to show those bigoted full-bloods that we're every bit as useful and viable a species and deserve to exist. At least, I hoped so. I hadn't met any other half-bloods yet, but I held out high hopes for our success.

"Colby? Hello? Colby Blanchard? Are you even listening to me?" Cyrus asked impatiently.

"Uh, sorry. What were you saying about the zone?"

He sighed in exasperation (he did that a lot with me) and repeated, "Since you refuse to allow me to test your skills in the evening, you have to be in the zone *all the time*."

I held up a hand to stop him. "Yeah, yeah, I get it. I'm sorry. It's just today is the day I meet my new sorority sisters and I'm really nervous."

"Oh, well then, that's fine. I'm sure no one will be out to get you today, then."

"Ha, ha," I retorted sarcastically.

"Today of all days you need to be most aware."

It took my Aunt Chloe exactly twelve minutes to tell Cyrus what I really was and persuade him to train me. Cyrus had believed her immediately, even though I walked around during the day and didn't have real fangs. I guess it was the incident about his grandmother that did it. I'd insisted on taking Bits to her doctor because she smelled different that day. My super sniffer detected a change in her normal lavender scent. It was a move that saved her life. Bits was on the verge of a heart attack, but thanks to me, she ended up with a bypass and a new lease on life.

He seemed to accept that I was a mutant Undead with limited vampiric powers who needed steel fangs to bite my victims because I had had my canine teeth removed for braces when I was twelve. I mean, it makes perfect sense, right? HA! It was my life and *I* had a hard time believing it most of the time.

"I wish you would let me teach you defense with weapons," he complained.

We were back to that old argument. I think he knew how close I was to caving on that one.

In the evenings, Thomas, my Vampire Investigator boyfriend, trained with me and we used swords. Actually, it would be fairer to say Thomas used the swords and I just did my best to avoid being beheaded and/or shish kebabed. Thomas wouldn't train me using a sword yet; he didn't think I was quite ready. Well, his actual words were something along the lines of "you'll poke your eye out" but the gist was the same.

I sighed heavily. "No, just help me avoid the stick."

He gave me his patented "you are one crazy chick" look and dropped the subject.

"Are you going to visit Bits today?" I asked.

"Already did. I have to leave tonight for a mission. I won't be back until Monday."

"You're leaving me?" I said in surprise.

"Yeah, I do have paying customers who need my services, you know. Don't worry, Thomas won't leave you alone this weekend. You should be fine."

"You know, I don't need Thomas's protection to be just fine. I can take care of myself."

"Oh really? Check out your shirt."

I glanced down to see a white chalk mark dead center in my chest. When I looked back at Cyrus, he held out the "wooden stake" for me to examine. It was really a large stick of chalk.

"Oh," I said in surprise, realizing if he was really out to get me, he could have killed me right then.

"You were saying?"

His constant superior ways and arrogance were always annoying, but today he was particularly obnoxious.

"Bite me," I replied in my snarkiest tone. Yes, I am the queen of maturity when provoked.

"That's your department," he said dryly and turned to walk away. Looking back over his shoulder, he added, "Be safe and don't hesitate to finish the job."

I watched him leave, his body tightly wound, ready to spring if the situation warranted it.

"He's so weird," commented a voice from behind, effectively scaring the daylights out of me.

"Aargh! Don't *do* that! You could've given me a heart attack!" I squealed, grabbing my chest for dramatic effect.

"The day your heart starts beating . . . I'll be the one having a heart attack."

Piper Prescott was my best friend and occasional arch nemesis. She wore her hair straight to the shoulders, jet-black with burgundy ends. Her nose was pierced, her skin a shade of alabaster rarely found on another living being and she always, always spoke her mind. We were direct opposites in so many ways but I wouldn't trade our friendship for all the Kate Spade bags in Macy's. Well, usually I felt that way.

"Dude, you are so funny, I forgot to laugh."

We moved to tidy up the recycling that Cyrus had scattered and walked into Piper's house to wash our hands.

"So, today's the big day, huh?" she asked after folding up the dish towel.

"Yep, tonight I meet the rest of the house. I can't believe it. You're gonna be there, right?" I was nervous about meeting them but proud of my accomplishment at the same time. I'd spent the last year of my life preparing for the moment I would meet the first half-bloods allowed to exist in vampire history. All because of me.

I knew that the Tribunal was sending me at least three new girls, if not more. One from as far away as Europe.

"Oh, I'll be there." Piper smirked. "Wouldn't miss it for the world."

"Do you have to be so negative?" I asked her. Piper was of the opinion that a bunch of girls with nothing in common except being Undead and forced to live together was a recipe for catastrophe.

She opened the fridge and took out a Mountain Dew. "I'm just saying this thing has disaster written all over it."

She tried to open the can but couldn't get her finger under the tab.

"Oh here, give it to me." I used my manicured nail to pop open her soda. "Are you still biting your nails?" I started to lecture, and then gasped when I noticed two of her cuticles had been chewed to the point of bleeding. "Piper! Your poor fingers. You've got to stop that!"

Piper put her hands over her ears and started to sing, "La la la la, I can't hear you, la la la."

"Oh fine." Piper usually resisted my suggestions for self-improvement. She'd always bitten her nails. Since kindergarten, when she was bored or stressed, she nibbled at them. I guess having a best friend who was a half-vampire that no Undead liked was a bit of a stressor.

I returned her drink and brought the conversation back to

my meeting. "And tonight doesn't have disaster written all over it. These girls are lucky to be alive and I bet they are just as excited to meet me as I am to meet them. After all, I *saved* them. Because of me, they get a second chance. You'll see."

We plopped down on a comfy couch in her living room, enjoying the air-conditioning for a moment.

"You seem awfully confident they are going to be happy with this arrangement. If I recall, you weren't all that thrilled with being attacked and turned into a vampire. What if the Tribunal told you that now you had to move across the country and learn the vampire ways?" Piper made it sound like vampires were part of the Dark Side or something.

"Of course I wasn't happy but I would rather be sent to Psi Phi House than be 'relieved of my Undead status.' And I'd be pretty darn thrilled to meet the person who was responsible for me getting a second chance to live as well."

Piper looked at me unconvinced and took a sip of her drink, so I gave up and changed the subject.

"Where's your mom?"

"She's still at work. We only have a couple of days left until we go to Europe. Even though she is dragging us on a work thing, I'm kind of excited. I miss England," she added wistfully.

Piper'd spent a summer with her family roaming the European countryside and loved it. She was kind of a gypsy at heart.

"You'll still be on e-mail, right? I know your cell phone won't work over there, but you'll still have Internet access, right?"

"Quit being so nervous. You'll be fine," Piper reassured me.

"Yeah, I know." I started to nibble on the cuticle of my thumb.

"I saw that Thomas was over last night. Is he finally putting out?" Piper asked.

"Piper! What kind of question is that?" I gasped, feigning outrage.

"So that would be a no, then."

I debated playing the offended victim but frankly, I needed some advice on this one. "What's wrong with me? We're in constant physical contact. He wrestles with me at training and I'm all, yeah baby come and get it, but he's been a perfect gentleman. It's starting to tick me off."

Thomas and I met eight months ago when he arrived at my house the night after I was attacked and turned into one of the Undead. He was a Vampire Investigator and it was his job to take care of any unlicensed vampires, like myself. And not "take care of" in the good sort of way. But Thomas fell for me and I have to admit, I fell for him as well. At least, as soon as I determined he wasn't going to stake me on our next date.

So it seemed natural once I attained my license that we should continue seeing each other. Except, I was given a stupid job with the Tribunal as half-blood Protector, which meant Thomas and I worked together now. He always takes his job way too seriously—instead of moonlit kisses and walks in the park we spent our free time training so I could be better *at my job*.

In the last eight months we rarely went on official "dates"

but he did hold my hand on the way to the training center and we exchanged a fair amount of kisses, but not much beyond that. Which was driving me insane!

"I sense a little frustration coming from the Blanchard household," Piper remarked dryly.

I scrunched up my nose, holding my thumb and forefinger up, about an inch apart. "Little bit."

"So why not just ask him what the deal is?"

"It's not that simple. He's old-fashioned and obsessed with training me. Like, totally obsessed. It's on his mind constantly. The other day I was in my knit bikini. You know, the purple one? It's totally scandalous!

"Anyway, I'm all prancin' around trying to get his mind off of training and he goes and gives me his sweatshirt to wear, so I won't get cold in the drafty warehouse we work out in. Ohmigod, he doesn't even ask why the hell I'm wearing a purple knit bikini to practice or anything, just covers me up and is all business. I must truly disgust him." I finished my tirade with a wail of self-pity.

"Wow."

I punch the sofa cushion next to me.

"Yeah, wow."

"You must look pretty bad in that bikini."

"Piper!"

She laughed at me. Did I mention Piper can be my arch nemesis *while* she is being my best friend?

"Okay, okay. First of all. Let's think a little, shall we? It's the middle of freakin' August and he gives you a sweatshirt to cover up with so you won't get cold? Hello? It's like, seventy degrees at night. He wanted you covered up because he obviously didn't trust himself to keep it in his pants if he had access to all that naked skin." I hadn't thought of it in those terms before and perked up at the thought of Thomas fearing he would lose control around me.

Piper continued her assessment. "Second, Thomas cares for you a lot. He's been training you hard so you can protect yourself. He doesn't want to lose you. And finally, maybe he's gay?"

I threw the pillow at Piper's head. No guy who kisses a girl like Thomas does could be gay. End of story.

"The last one must be it," I jokingly agreed with her, not completely convinced but feeling much better about things.

After a moment of companionable silence, Piper said "Colby?"

"Yeah?"

"Quit chewing on your nails."

Brat.

TWO

Once dusk made an appearance, Piper and I headed over to my new home. The sorority house was located at the end of Greek Rowe, just a couple of blocks from Puget Sound University. Though PSU was a smaller college, it boasted three other sororities and four frats.

I'd spent the summer with the interior decorator hired by the Tribunal. She was a perfectly respectable vampire who bordered on uptight. At first, she seemed to dislike me as much as other vampires but after working together on the house plans, she warmed up. Well, warmed as much as an Undead can. The only point we disagreed on was the amount of pink in the house. Shades of pink were the house colors so I really thought it needed to make a statement.

Piper parked in the designated "President's Space," which

I'm not ashamed to admit gave me a thrill. We hopped out of the car and I insisted we wait for Thomas on the sunporch before entering.

"Why are we waiting for tall, dead and handsome? Didn't you at least let *him* see the house before now?" Piper whined.

"No, I wanted all of us to see it together. I want both of your reactions at the same time. I worked really hard on the color scheme, furniture, spaces. All of it."

"Fine," Piper huffed, plopping down in a wicker rocking chair. "You mind telling me what vampires are going to be enjoying the sunporch? Because it is, ya know, a *sun*porch?"

"Just because you would sit on the porch during the day doesn't mean everyone else has to. Besides, the girls might be able to be out during the day, like me."

"Might? As in you don't know?"

I squirmed a bit at her line of questioning. I really didn't want to admit I knew practically nothing about any of the people arriving this evening, especially to Piper. "Well, I don't have all their vampire attributes committed to memory."

"Hmmm," she said, looking at me speculatively.

Luckily, Thomas arrived at that moment so I was able to divert Piper's attention to the house once again. I jumped up and gave him a quick kiss.

"Hi honey, ready to see my masterpiece?" I pulled the keys out of my pocket.

"Of course." He smiled warmly at me and I sort of melted into a pool of lust, figuratively speaking of course.

"Piper." He nodded a greeting her way.

"Hey," Piper returned.

"Okay." I started my grand tour. "As you both know I've been working with the decorator on the house, and though we disagreed a bit on the color scheme, things really took shape.

"Outside the house you'll note our sorority letters"— ΨΦ—"which stands for Psi Phi House!" I couldn't help but giggle again at the name. After all, how cute was I to pick out Psi Phi since it was pronounced Sci-Fi? A sorority for vampires called Psi Phi. Get it? I crack myself up.

I looked to my captive audience for their reaction, which appeared to be proper awe. Excellent. "Moving on inside the house"—I put the key in the lock and pushed the door open— "we enter the foyer, and directly to the right is our living room."

I stepped aside, letting Thomas and Piper catch the full effect of my decorating influences. The walls were washed with a soft blush color, while the sectional couches were soft pink with a dark pink trim. To break up the monochromatic color palette, the decorator added accent touches of khaki, such as the floral print in the curtains and throw rugs over the hardwood.

"Well? What do you think?"

"It's, uh, very true to the house colors," Thomas said in a diplomatic way.

"It looks like Barbie threw up in here," Piper stated flatly.

"What do you mean?!" I exclaimed.

"It's pink!" Piper explained, as though talking to a child.

"Duh, I know it's pink. The house colors are pink and blush. Sheesh, don't you ever listen when I'm talking to you?"

She shot me a look that I interpreted as "rarely" so I addressed Thomas instead.

"Don't you think it's cozy?" I walked over and plopped down on the overstuffed sectional, beckoning him to join me. Thomas hesitated a moment before moving in my direction, careful not to disturb the vase of silk lilies next to me, and sitting down. Well, actually it was more like he drowned in the cushions.

"What the—?!" he exclaimed, struggling to right himself.

"That's the style of the couch. It's made to sort of melt with your body so you can veg."

He managed to perch himself on the corner of the sofa, teetering precariously with a pained expression on his face.

"You don't like it," I accused him.

"I didn't say that," he started to defend himself.

"Colby, I want to see the rest of the house," Piper interrupted, casting dubious looks around the room as though half expecting the pink furniture to come alive and swallow her.

"Fine." I rolled myself off the couch (there is an art to getting out of a squishy sofa, you know) and continued playing tour guide.

"To the left you have our formal dining room." My hand swept toward a room painted a khaki shade with a deep pink trim. The table was very large, seating at least twelve in a very formal setting.

"Why do you have a dining room?" Piper asked.

"Because it's a house. Duh."

"Yeah, but a house full of people who don't eat food."

"So? Everyone else doesn't know we don't eat food. We have to keep up appearances," I said in exasperation. Piper threw up her hands in defeat as we continued into the kitchen.

This room was large, with a nice island in the middle and was stocked with the latest gourmet cookware. Sure, we wouldn't have any food in the pantry, but it was a pretty nifty kitchen, nonetheless.

"Whose room is this back here?" Piper asked.

"That belongs to the housemother," I told her. It was a moderately sized room, furnished with a bed, desk and television and its own private bathroom.

"Who's the housemother?" Thomas asked, concern radiating in his voice.

"I thought I'd bring in a vampire slayer," I retorted sarcastically. "At this point, no one. I mean, who am I going to choose to play the role of Undead housemother? I don't think any full-blood is going to jump at the job, and I wouldn't want one here anyway." I looked at Thomas meaningfully. "You're not a trustworthy lot."

Then I caressed his cheek with my hand, smiling as I said it so he knew I didn't really include him in my opinions of the vampire population.

"Good to know, thanks." He smiled back. I caught a glimpse of his dimple and wanted to throw him down on the bed but Piper was in the room and Thomas—well, Thomas would completely freak out over my forwardness. Sighing deeply, I continued playing Tour Guide Barbie.

"Directly up the stairs is my room." They obediently followed me to the second level. I had my own bathroom and would be sleeping in the bedroom itself. The other girls would be sleeping in the dorm room and keeping their stuff in their assigned bedrooms.

"Where do the other girls sleep?" Piper asked, after looking in each room and finding the group bathroom.

"Ah, that would be in the basement. I'll show you."

We had just started our descent down the stairs when the doorbell rang.

"But first, I will get the door and greet my fellow sisters." I bounded down the remaining stairs, nervous and excited at the same time. How would it go? Would they fall over themselves in gratitude? That could be a little embarrassing but understandable. I mean, I did save their lives and all.

"Here it goes," I said with a smile and swung open the door. What greeted me was a sight I was unprepared for, to say the least: a very large man, who didn't strike me as a vampire, wearing an official-looking police uniform complete with gun and wooden stakes on his belt. His badge said "Tribunal Security."

"Can I help you?" I asked nervously, glancing around his wide frame in hopes of finding my new roommates.

"Are you Colby Blanchard?" he asked matter-of-factly.

I took a defensive step back and replied, "Who wants to know?"

"I have a delivery for Colby Blanchard at this address. I need a signature." He offered me an electronic signature thing that the FedEx people always had and gestured for me to sign it.

Totally confused, I took it from his hand and obediently signed my name with flourish. Maybe the Tribunal forgot to deliver something for the House? Perhaps a lovely, expensive welcome present that required security to deliver it? I perked up at the thought of an ancient piece of artwork to commemorate this auspicious occasion.

Buff Guy took back the signature pad and gestured to the street. To my shock and horror, the back of a relatively inconspicuous van swung open and two people were literally thrown from the back, handcuffed and bedraggled. A second security guard jumped out behind them, and with a third, who must have opened the door because I didn't see him at first, escorted the prisoners—as I could think of nothing else to call them—onto the sunporch.

I gaped at Thomas, who wore a concerned look, and Piper, who merely raised her eyebrow in surprise as the women were prodded into the house.

"What the hell is going on here?" I demanded when I could finally find my voice. They were treating these half-bloods like felons!

The guy I addressed looked at me in confusion. "I'm bringing you the half-blood prisoners."

"They aren't prisoners, you idiot! They're free. Free to come and go, free to live their Undead existence, they're just plain *free*. Thomas?" I looked to him for guidance.

Thomas stepped forward and pulled out his identification badge, flashing it to the surprised rent-a-cop.

"I'll take it from here," he said, waiting for the guy to understand he was a Tribunal Investigator aka half-blood persecutor. Well, at least he was until the law changed. Now he spent his time training me and chasing rogue vampires.

"An Investigator, huh?" The guy motioned his team to bring the girls into the house. He looked around and took in the furnishings, colors, and then glanced toward me again. "Are you sure this isn't an interrogation facility?"

"Interrogation facility?" I asked him quietly and Thomas put a restraining hand on my arm. My voice had gone very calm, a sure sign I was about to lose it. I'm in total control when I'm squawking like an enraged chicken but when I get all quiet and focused, that is the time to back away from the crazy blonde chick.

The guy must have sensed I was ready to spring because he decided to backtrack. "My orders were to bring these two half-bloods here and usually we take them to . . ."

I saw Thomas making a cutting gesture across his throat to silence the guard from sharing too much information; when I turned toward him, he pretended he was batting away a fly.

"You take them to where?" I asked again, my eyes still on Thomas.

"To a facility for interrogation." The security guard was

definitely uncomfortable, anxious to drop off his parcels and hit the road. I think he sensed a storm brewing and wanted to get the heck out of Dodge before it hit.

At this point Piper spoke up. "Where's their stuff?"

"Stuff?" the guard standing next to our new guests asked.

"Yeah, stuff. Things like clothes, luggage, cosmetics, scrapbooks, memorabilia. You know, stuff."

"They don't have any stuff," he said, clearly confused.

Exasperated, I turned around and walked up to the girls, who were still handcuffed, and gasped in horror. They were gagged as well.

"Give me the keys," I demanded and when he was slow to cooperate I looked him in the eyes and powered all my Undead mojo into the next order. "The keys, now."

Instantly, he handed them over to me as though in a trance; when I snatched them away, he looked confused and bewildered. As though he had no idea why he'd given them to me in the first place.

I unlocked each girl and they immediately rubbed their wrists, but didn't try to remove the tape across their mouths. Both were still cowed in the presence of the Tribunal security.

"I am so sorry for this . . ." I apologized to them as I yanked the duct tape off. It was obvious that so far, I made a crappy Protector, but I had the role of sadistic mustache waxer down to a science.

"Beat it," I told the two guards and they immediately stepped away and headed toward the door.

"Are you sure . . . ?" The mouthpiece for the group was

a little hesitant, obviously uncomfortable in our pink foyer.

I looked over my shoulder and growled in his direction. My eyes were aglow and brilliant yellow, my teeth bared with what I hoped was ferocious dominance. Sadly, I don't have fangs like other vampires so I was sure instead of looking intimidating and frightening, I looked crazy and disturbed. Either way, the guy really didn't want to tangle with me.

Thomas assured him everything was fine and they left.

Piper immediately broke the tension by mocking me.

"What was that? Was that supposed to be intimidating? Were you striking fear in the hearts of men?" She shook her head. "No wonder the guy thinks this is a half-blood loony bin."

"You are soooo not helping." I sighed in exasperation.

All of a sudden, one of the cowering prisoners launched herself at me, knocking both of us to the floor. She was surprisingly strong, grabbing my hair and slamming my head into the hardwood floors. After a moment of stunned horror I rolled over and pinned her beneath me, trying to get her subdued and my hair free.

She was completely going bonkers, hair-snatching and screaming at me in Spanish. I recognized *puta* from my first year Spanish class (because really, the first thing you ever learn in a foreign language class is how to curse) and a string of other words spoken too quickly for me to grasp. All in all, I couldn't really blame her with how she'd been treated to this point. When she managed to punch me in the face, however, I decided enough was enough. No more nice Protector.

Three

straddled her, knees on either side of her waist and, using a good dose of strength, I grabbed her by the shoulders and slammed her down into the hardwood.

"There will be no fighting in the crazy er, sorority house!" I screamed, correcting myself in frustration.

She stopped struggling as she fought to maintain consciousness. I rolled off her to get a good look at her and give her a chance to catch her breath.

She was Latin, obviously, if the colorful Spanish vocabulary didn't give her away. My first guess was Mexican. She had great skin color, even though she was Undead. Dirty, tired and a mess, I could tell she was still very pretty. Voluptuous, much like Piper, but shorter. An Undead Salma Hayek. No doubts what the vampire who changed her had in mind.

I looked up at the other girl, who was trembling, trying to look invisible in the big pink room. She was wearing her pajamas with, get this, fuzzy bunny slippers. I groaned inwardly, praying she was at least legal age.

Piper moved toward her and introduced herself. "Hi, I'm Piper. That's Thomas and the crazy chick rolling on the floor with your friend is Colby." She smiled at the girl, who seemed a little less afraid because Piper was making fun of me and—well, it *was* rather funny that I was rolling on the floor with a wild Mexican Lolita.

The girl tentatively took Piper's hand and said, "I'm Lucy Meyers."

"It's very nice to meet you, Lucy," Piper replied, clasping her hand in a firm handshake.

"She's not going to hurt me, is she?" Lucy asked Piper, her cornflower blue eyes looking huge in her pale gaunt face, and I groaned. It was like Bambi thought I was gonna make her into venison or something.

"Well, don't go nuts and try to pound her skull into the ground and I think you two will get along just fine." Piper smirked at me, keeping the conversation light but making it clear that I was defending myself against an attacker and not randomly knocking people unconscious.

Lucy smiled tentatively and I smiled back. Then Piper added, "People are always launching themselves at Colby. She brings out the best in them that way. You'll get used to it."

Lucy giggled into her hand.

"Hardy-har-har. You're a scream today, Piper." I stood up and dusted off my backside.

"You're not what I expected," Lucy said shyly after shaking my hand.

"Really? What did you expect?" I asked, intrigued by what kinds of rumors were circulating about me.

"Someone older," she confessed and then clarified, "Not that you're not old enough to be the Protector, it's just . . ."

"Ah, so you know who I am. Don't sweat the old thing. I'm gonna look this way forever so I could be much older than I appear."

"I'm sorry. I've been locked away a very long time and my manners are rusty. I'm so grateful you are, well, you." She smiled with such sincerity I admit I felt my chest puff out a bit in pride. Now we were getting somewhere. This was the kind of reception I planned on, not being attacked by someone I was supposed to protect.

"You said you've been locked away? I don't understand." Piper interrupted the lovefest with her question.

"I can't explain it myself. After I was attacked and changed, I was taken away to a place I can only describe as a kind of prison. They fed me and let me watch TV and stuff but I was there all alone for months before Angie joined me and then we were transported here."

I looked at Thomas in question. Only an Investigator could have placed her in a holding cell.

"It's possible, since there was nowhere for her to go. The

house wasn't ready yet and it wouldn't be safe for her in the vampire world."

The mysterious Angie took that moment to moan from the floor. I needed her to understand I wasn't going to harm her, if she would only stop pulling my hair long enough to listen. I reached down for her hands to pull her up. This time she didn't struggle and I helped her to her feet.

"Let's try this again," I said slowly, looking her in the eyes. "My name is Colby and I won't hurt you. Do you understand? Just don't go pulling my hair again and we'll be fine. What's your name?"

She looked around the room, a hunted desperation in her eye but when nothing happened she relaxed a little and said, "My name is Angelina Flores."

"Great, well it's nice to meet you, Angie?" I looked at her for confirmation that she used Angie as a nickname and she nodded. "Welcome to Psi Phi House, your new home away from home."

I gestured around the room, proud to finally be showing my people all I had done for them. She looked around dubiously. I must have been wearing an expectant look on my face, because she felt obligated to give her opinion.

"It's pink," she stated, less than enthusiastically. Piper laughed and Thomas coughed. I glared at them and he tried covering his mouth again but his shoulders were shaking. She took one look at my face and backpedaled quickly.

"I like pink. Pink is . . ." She took another desperate look around the room and finished lamely, "Pink."

I sighed heavily. "You don't have to lie to me, I'm not gonna lock you up if you don't like pink. But you are gonna have to get used to it 'cause the pink stays," I said firmly. I certainly didn't want to give anyone the idea that I was willing to change my house colors in some sort of democratic vote or something.

She nodded in agreement, then asked, "Is every room pink?"

"You're welcome to check it all out and see for yourself. First let me show you to the sleeping room and then you can pick out your bedrooms."

Everyone followed me back toward the library, which was located across the hall from the housemother's room. It looked like an ordinary library, with two wingback reading chairs and walls lined with bookcases.

I walked into the room and stopped in front of the far bookcase. I found a big red book and pushed it forward; the bookcase made a clicking sound, popping out just a bit. I pulled it open the rest of the way using the hidden handle in the side of the door frame, and voilà, a secret staircase.

"Cool," Piper couldn't help but murmur and I noticed the rest of the group nodded. Yeah, I thought of that, thankyouverymuch.

The light flipped on automatically and they followed me down the stairs to a huge basement. It was divided into two rooms. One was the sleeping dorm, with bunkbeds lining the walls. A partition separated the dorm in the center, giving the quarters a little more privacy.

The other half of the room was a place for everyone to

kick back and relax. Plasma screen television and couches for chilling, a large conference table and chairs for house meetings and homework. There were even a couple of computers for the girls to surf the Web and check e-mail.

"It's not pink!" exclaimed Angie, who seemed delighted with the warm, inviting earth tones.

"Yeah, well, I had to throw the decorator a bone." *Or she might have tried to suck me dry*, I added to myself wryly.

In the sleeping room, the colors changed again. The beds all had coordinating comforters and accessories in blue and lavender. Then on the other side of the partition the room colors changed to pale yellow and green. See, I could be reasonable about the pink.

I let them walk around and just soak it all in, feeling a huge amount of pride in my work. It was all coming together now. My dream was finally becoming a reality.

"Colby?" Lucy questioned apologetically. "Is there somewhere we can clean up?"

I smacked my hand against my forehead, "Dude, I am so stupid. Of course you wanna take a shower and stuff. I suck. Sure, the bathrooms and showers are upstairs. There are robes and towels up there too. Let me show you."

I walked them back upstairs and pointed out where the trial-size shampoos and such were. I figured most people would bring their own stuff but was glad my mom suggested having some travel sizes on hand. Moms think of everything.

"They're going to need clean clothes," Piper said, once they were in the shower.

"Yeah, they don't have anything. Thomas, why is that?"

We both turned to stare at him, as though it were his fault since he was a Vampire Investigator and all.

"I have no idea. They should have been escorted with all their belongings. This is a safe house, not a prison. I'm going to call my supervisor and see if I can't get the details of their relocation."

He flipped open his cell phone and wandered downstairs, speaking into it and completely ignoring us.

"Well, he's nothing if not efficient," Piper said to me after he was gone.

"You have no idea," I answered, rolling my eyes heavenward. When he was on task, nothing and I mean *nothing* could stray him from his goal. Not even a purple knit bikini.

"Who's open this late?" I said.

"Hmm, the malls are closed but Wal-Mart is probably still open, or Fred Meyer?"

Not two of the most appealing options but hey, beggars couldn't be choosers. Especially if the goal was clean underwear.

"Piper, could you . . . ?" I started to ask.

"Yeah, yeah, I'm on it. Underwear, some sweats and tank tops? Something for a little support 'cause I'm not guessing bra sizes or anything."

"You're a gem," I said as I grabbed my purse. I pulled out a hundred-dollar bill. My mom and dad had given me emergency spending money before I left today and I was already using it. I promised myself that I would get reimbursed from the

Tribunal for the undies and any new clothes the girls needed. This was their fault anyway.

She took the money and said, "I'm buying myself some dinner too. I'm starving." And with that sentiment, she loped down the stairs like a good little errand girl. I don't know what I would do without Piper. Sure, she was a pain in the backside but when push came to shove, there was no one else I would rather have in my corner.

Of course, there was one other person who I wouldn't mind having in my corner. I stopped at the bottom stair watching Thomas pace the back hallway, phone to his ear, occasionally nodding or asking a question. His brow was furrowed in concentration and I had an overwhelming urge to take his phone and start kissing away the worry lines.

Instead I waited patiently, wondering what was wrong with me that he didn't want to take our relationship to the next level. Was my butt too big? Too small? Maybe my shoulder-length blonde hair wasn't long enough?

Suddenly, I had a horrifying thought. Did my breath stink? I cupped my hand in front of my mouth and tried to exhale, but practically passed out from dizziness instead. I looked up in time to see Thomas staring at me with the oddest expression, much like the one I wore whenever I witnessed Piper wearing ratty Converses with new jeans. Hello? Ever hear of a pair of wedges? But then again, who was I to judge? I just freaked out over the thought of having bad breath and I don't even breathe!

"Good news," Thomas said, snapping his phone shut.

"I could use some."

"Looks like all the other half-bloods should be here within the hour, with luggage. I don't know what the deal was with Lucy and Angie but it seems like they were the only problem. I'm still checking into why they were taken into custody to begin with, I should get some answers soon."

"Well, I guess that's good news. I sent Piper out to buy them some unmentionables, but they'll need real clothes. I think I know just the person to help me out."

As I walked toward the living room, Thomas stepped behind me, curious as to my plan. I phoned the Tribunal Offices and Mrs. Durham answered.

"Tribunal," she answered in a very professional way.

"Hey Margaret, it's me, Colby."

I could feel the deep freeze through the phone. Did I mention Mrs. Durham hated to be called by her first name? Oh yeah, almost as much as she hated me.

"He's not taking any calls right now," she said very coolly.

I rolled my eyes in response, but remembered she couldn't see me. She was always telling me that Mr. Holloway was unavailable.

"No problem. Look, I have a problem over here that I need fixed." I thought I would start out taking the high road, well, except for the fact that I tried to get her goat right out of the gate by calling her Margaret.

"So," she drawled.

I gritted my teeth. "Soooo, I thought you might have the power to help me out. I mean, I know Mr. Holloway will do it for me but since his time is so valuable and all . . ." Did I mention that Mrs. Durham considered herself the gatekeeper to the top three vampires in the Tribunal? She was all about making herself indispensable.

"What do you need?" She was back to being the crisp professional.

"Well, I have a couple of sorority members that lost their luggage in transport and are going to need the works. So, we need an evening at Nordstrom or something. Tribunal footing the bill, of course."

"What?!" Ol' Margaret hated me for two reasons. One, Mr. Holloway, who was one of *the* three vampires in the Tribunal, always helped me out and that bugged her. But what bugged her more was the fact that I was a half-blood allowed to live.

"Yeah, I know we have one or two Undead on the board over there, so we need the place opened an extra hour so my gals can pick up the essentials."

"Absolutely not," she practically screeched.

"Oh yeah," I continued as though she hadn't said a word, "they're going to need a shopping chaperone as well. Someone who takes care of the billing details. Only that person would really know who bought what so they would pretty much have a free reign shopping as well."

There was a long pause at the other end of the line. Oh yeah, she didn't wear St. John's knit suits with Beverly Feldman shoes and not recognize the opportunity of a lifetime dumped into her lap. It might go against the grain to help out half-bloods but she could pick up what she wanted in the process, so what was a little greasing the wheels between enemies?

"Fine. I'll do it. But only this once. I'll set it up for the end of next week."

"Set it up for tomorrow night. I'll have them meet you at the concierge service desk at closing. Thank you, *Margaret*."

I heard the decisive click of being hung up on and then the loud buzzing of the dial tone, trying its best to sound rude as well. I had to admit that Margaret Durham brought out the worst in me. It was childish to treat her like that but I'd spent the summer playing it nice, trying to get her to like me, and in return she kept me waiting for hours when I had an appointment with Mr. Holloway *and* she deliberately messed up the construction time lines so the house took twice as long to complete. She was a bigot to the bone and I decided I wasn't going to let her yank my chain anymore.

"Mrs. Durham is not a vampire you want as an enemy. She holds a position of power with the Tribunal," Thomas tried to warn me.

"Dude, she answers their phones. She's not all that. Anyway, Mr. Holloway isn't going to let her get away with harming me or this project," I assured him haughtily.

"Why is that, exactly?" Thomas prodded, not for the first time.

I didn't like this part. The part in our relationship where I kept secrets from Thomas. I mean, there are secrets, like how much you really weigh, and secrets, like I killed Holloway's rogue vampire son and now I'd kind of taken his place in the family. No one knew that Charles Winthrop, the rogue vampire who changed me into an Undead, was really the son of Tribunal leader C.W. Holloway. Well, almost no one. I kept his secret and he created the half-blood training and reintroduction into vampire society program.

"Guess he just feels bad for persecuting my people for hundreds of years." I gave Thomas my best innocent smile and he grunted at me. I don't think he was buying it but he could hardly accuse me of lying about the intentions of the leader of our vampire society, now could he?

It was at that moment that the front doorbell rang. And rang again. And rang yet again before I could even get the ten feet to the door. Sheesh, hold your horses already.

I opened the door, ready to chew out the overambitious doorbell ringer when the sight that greeted me actually struck me speechless. And I can tell you that rarely, if ever, happens.

On the porch sat a dozen or so suitcases, trunks, hatboxes and totes practically over-flowing with stuff. On the curb was a—could it be? Yes it was—a white limousine with dignitary flags flapping in the night breeze.

I counted at least four men scrambling to remove even more stuff from the car and helping someone onto the sunporch. Thomas stood behind me and I felt him shudder at the amount of luggage our new resident had brought.

"Ileana Margaret Mary Mircea Romanav," Thomas whispered in my ear.

"Is that your idea of sweet talk?" I asked him, half-joking.

"Uh, no. That's the name of your new guest. She is part

British, part Romanian and it appears she is also part of the royal family."

"You know, when the Tribunal sent the message out that we would train other clans' half-bloods I didn't think Romania would crate up one of their nobility and ship them to us."

Thomas nodded in agreement. It was very odd indeed. It didn't look as though Ms. Romanav wanted for any material comforts. Compared to how Lucy and Angie arrived, that had my half-blood senses tingling. Something was not right here.

We didn't have time for any more discussion as the person in question sashayed up the concrete steps and announced herself.

"I am Ileana Romanav. Who is in charge here?" Her gaze swept past me in immediate dismissal and landed on Thomas. When her face softened into charmed delight it took all my self-control not to go medieval on her noble self.

"I am." I stepped forward to shake her hand, which she didn't immediately take because she seemed unable to comprehend that Thomas was not introducing himself and welcoming her inside.

I stood there, with my hand extended for what seemed like eternity. I repeated, loudly, "I am. Welcome to Psi Phi House, Ileana. My name is Colby Blanchard and this is my boyfriend, Thomas."

She seemed to snap out of her daze at the mention of "boyfriend" and looked at me once again. This time taking a moment to really see me.

Sure, my hair was blonde and straight, stopping just past

my shoulders and her hair was a honey gold with spiral curls
that seemed to go on forever. I can say that I didn't feel intim-
idated by her porcelain pale skin, or her Mediterranean green
eyes, which I doubted had anything to do with colored contacts. Nope, I'm sure she was checking me out and wishing
she had a few freckles to break up the monotony of a flawless
complexion and admiring my glowing yellow eyes. Okay,
who am I kidding? She was fab and I felt drab. Gee, I hated
her already.

She stared at my hand as though I were offering a snake
for inspection.

"I see." She gave a tight little smile. "This trip has simply
exhausted me, could you kindly show me to my suite?"

"Suite?" I asked, pulling my hand back in distracted confusion. Wow, the luggage just kept coming out of the back of
the car. It reminded me of the scene in *Mary Poppins* when
Julie Andrews kept pulling limitless things from her amazing
carpetbag.

"Yes, suite." She frowned at me and spoke more slowly.
"My apartment for my visit."

At the word "visit," Thomas and I exchanged a look.

"You have a room, which you will be sharing with two
other sisters. There is no suite."

"No suite?" It was her time to sound confused.

"I'm afraid not."

"But what about my things?" She gestured to the growing
mound of stuff accumulating around her.

"We can probably store most of it, since you brought it with you. Some of the other girls arrived with slightly less, uh, stuff so we might be able to pack most of it in the back room." Heck, we didn't have a housemother so we could use that room for the time being.

"Pack it away?! Oh no, that simply won't do. I brought only my essentials. I need all of it."

"I see," I murmured, beginning to realize that Ms. Romanav was fast becoming a pain in my backside I didn't really need right now.

"Might I suggest you give Ileana a tour of the house while her men wait with the luggage and then we can make an informed decision on where to put her things?" Thomas politely suggested, the eternal diplomat.

"Agreed." Ileana clapped her hands in enthusiasm. I stepped back and she immediately moved forward, taking Thomas's arm and entering Psi Phi House. I was effectively placed in the role of tour guide, again. She spoke little through the tour of the main floor, merely nodding as I showed each room, her face carefully masked to show only polite interest.

The veneer cracked upon entering the upstairs bedrooms, when I reminded her that House rules indicated she wouldn't be sleeping in the room, merely housing her clothes and things with two other girls.

"This simply won't do. I brought my housemaid Sophie and she stays with me at all times."

We looked at each other, both of us waiting for the other

to back down, while Thomas uneasily shifted his weight back and forth on his feet. His obvious unease punctured my stubbornness. I realized I was the one in charge. It was up to me, the Protector, to play diplomat and make this situation work. Sometimes being in charge bites.

"Ileana, why don't you pick out a room? We'll put your luggage, trunks and such downstairs to store in the housemother's room. I believe we will have enough space in the beginning that Sophie may have a room as well; you could store your additional clothes and such with her."

"Very well," she agreed, noting my tight smile. She probably sensed that was as much as I was going to offer. Smart girl. Obvious pain in the butt, but smart. And she should be satisfied because she now had two rooms to store her things. That might not be a suite, but it was more than everyone else had.

Four

"Tell me why you're a pickup service again?"

I grabbed my lightweight sweater from the coatrack and my purse while Thomas walked to the door.

"You saw how Lucy and Angie arrived? Thomas was checking into it when he discovered there are two half-bloods being held in some house in Paradise Point, California. The person who has them refuses to give them up. Piper, they are probably chained in some dark basement somewhere having God knows what done to them. We're going to free them and bring them back."

Piper still didn't look convinced, or impressed.

"So why can't Thomas go get them? Why do you have to go? And more importantly, why do I have to stay and babysit Psi Phi House?" She definitely needed more convincing.

"Because we want to get in and get out and to do that, it would be easier to free them during the day. You know, when the vampires are sleeping? Thomas knows the area and has the credentials. Also, he's Blooded and other vamps listen to him." I looked toward him dubiously. "Well, that's his theory anyway."

"So you guys are grabbing a nocturnal flight, getting your captives and flying home tomorrow evening. You'll be back in no time?" It was weird to see Piper so jittery.

"Relax. Everything will be fine. The girls will sleep and all you have to do is make sure they get to Nordstrom on time. Mrs. Durham will meet you at the concierge desk and take everyone around. Get yourself something pretty. The Tribunal owes you a new outfit for helping me anyway." At least, *I* thought they did.

Thomas snapped his cell phone shut and spoke up. "Carl is on his way. He'll be with you until morning and back again for the shopping trip. I don't expect much activity during the day. You should be safe."

"Safe? You think I'm worried about being safe? These girls are whacked. And that snooty English chick is in a category all her own. I'm not worried about my safety. I'm worried about my *sanity*."

I grabbed both her shoulders and looked deep in her eyes. "I believe in you."

Then I sort of chucked her on the upper arm with my fist as a form of moral support and escaped Psi Phi House with

Thomas. To be honest, I was feeling more than a little bit relieved to get away from my new sorority sisters.

I'd expected things to be different. Well, to be honest, I expected things to be a lot different. I guess I was living in a bit of a fantasy world, assuming they would be grateful I'd brought them to college and under my wing, to learn the ways of the vampire world. They all seemed pretty annoyed to be there. And I couldn't blame them.

I certainly wasn't pleased when I was attacked and turned into the walking Undead, so throw in a relocate without any say in the matter and—whammo!—it's safe to say I had a house of ticked off sisters. And I was leaving them with Piper. I tried not to look back at her when I got into Thomas's car. She still stood at the doorway, staring in disbelief that I was actually leaving and worse still, leaving her in charge.

I made a mental note to pick her up a souvenir from Paradise Point. Something fun and beachy with shells to help make it up to her. Carl picked us up and we sped along to Sea-Tac International Airport to catch our flight into LAX. We still had a couple hours' drive ahead of us once we landed. Luckily it was a short flight; we should have plenty of time to get to a vampire safe house so Thomas didn't fry in the morning sun. Traveling with a full-blooded vampire really made vacationing a little less spontaneous.

Once we made it through security and onto the plane, it was time to get serious.

"So, tell me everything you know about this evil slave-trader vampire."

"Well, Cookie Flanneg—"

"Cookie? *Cookie?!* The evil slave trader's name is Cookie?" My voice raised an octave and the lady in front of us looked over the back of the seat disapprovingly.

"As I was saying, Cookie Flannegan"—he gave me a warning look when he saw the expression on my face—"runs a sort of resort for vacationing vampires. She has two half-blood slaves who she is apparently unwilling to release into our custody."

"What does she do with them?" I asked

"Unclear. She's had one for awhile now and recently acquired"—I snorted at his choice of words—"another."

"I thought it was illegal to make half-bloods."

"For the general vampire population, yes."

"But Cookie is an exception to the rule?"

"You have to understand that many vampires on the Council and in the Tribunal enjoy the hospitality of Cookie. She is somewhat of a favored full-blood. Certain allowances have been made. A sort of don't-ask-and-don't-tell policy."

"Okay, so say Mr. Holloway makes his way down to sunny California for a little R & R and gets his kicks at Ms. Cookie's Vampire Emporium. He sees some chained-up half-blood that's forced to do who knows what sort of evil and degrading things—he just turns a blind eye?" I was incredulous to say the least.

"I think we should reserve judgment until we have all the facts."

"The facts? We have the facts! Cookie the Creep is enslaving half-blood vampires and the Council doesn't care! In fact, they're all 'Hey Cookie, that's okay. Thanks for the good time.'"

Thomas looked at me with a half-smile.

"What?" I demanded, unnerved by his tender look.

"What?!" I demanded again, "Do I have dirt on my cheek?" I rubbed my face furiously with the palm of my hand.

"No, no dirt. It's your fervor. You get very passionate about your job. I like that."

He gently tucked a stray tendril behind my ear, sort of deflating my righteous anger. Now I just felt kind of gushy and warm and, if you must know, tingly in all the right places. What can I say? I'm not a complicated chick.

"Do we have a plan of attack?" I asked softly; my mouth felt kind of dry and woolen.

"First, let's get there and check into our room. Then, if there's time, we can go to the house. Otherwise, we'll wait until tomorrow night."

My whole body came alive at his mention of our sharing a room but I was immediately distracted when he suggested waiting until the next evening to do anything.

"Why can't I scout out the house during the day? There won't be any vampire activity and I might be able to talk to the hostages or free them on my own without a fight."

"We don't know what you'll be up against, so it's best to wait until both of us can check it out."

I leaned back in my seat, mouth dangling open in shock. I was the Protector of half-blood vampires for crying out loud and he didn't think I was capable of going to an Undead house *during the day* without screwing things up? I couldn't believe he thought so little of my skills that I couldn't be trusted to do a little recon.

He took my silence as agreement and leaned his head against the window to close his eyes and take a catnap. I fumed silently, stewing in resentment. Sure, I was on the assignment but Thomas wasn't going to let me do anything. He was just letting me tag along or, worse yet, had been *forced* to bring me along and really didn't want me here at all!

I was not going to wait meekly for the big, strong Vampire Investigator to save the world. That was my job. He could be the sidekick for a change. I was going in during the day.

* * *

We touched down two hours later with Thomas dozing most of the way. It didn't take much time to rent a car and head down the coast to Paradise Point. The plan (at least Thomas's plan) was to gather as much information as possible about Cookie and her beach house while waiting for darkness at the safe house. My plan was to leave Thomas napping and save the two half-bloods myself.

We arrived in Paradise Point in a little over two hours.

Thomas took us directly toward the ocean and we did a drive-by of the scenic beach homes.

"What are you doing?" I asked, wondering why we were sightseeing and not heading immediately to the safe house.

"Just trying to scope out the area," he answered in a non-committal way. I narrowed my eyes at him.

"You know, sunrise is gonna happen any minute now."

Which was a bit of an exaggeration on my part, but the man had a way of keeping secrets and pissing me off.

He reached over and patted my knee in a patronizing sort of way. "Don't worry about a thing," he said.

Can you believe he actually *said* that to me?! He might as well have said, "Don't worry your pretty little head about it." If I was having second thoughts about leaving him behind and rescuing the prisoners myself (and I might have been), his attitude at that moment sealed his fate. He was so being left behind in our room.

He wound down the long beach road and took a turn east toward a large two-story house, which I could only assume was the safe house. It looked like a sleepy residential area. Thomas drove around the back of the house and parked in a spacious gravel lot, next to a white Mercedes and silver Lexus. Say what you want about vampires, but being around for so long, they seemed to have mastered the material aspects of living.

I was surprised to discover the house was a split-level with a secluded half basement. We entered the back door and stepped into a small alcove, complete with reception desk.

Now this looked more like a cute bed-and-breakfast than a safe house. Though I really didn't know what I was expecting. After all, who goes to a safe house or even knows what one is supposed to look like anyway?

Thomas rang the bell and waited patiently, absently caressing my shoulder with his strong hand. He started to massage my neck and I practically purred with contentment until the check-in clerk bounded down the steps to our left and greeted us.

"Hello, Thomas!" the man's voice boomed. He was larger than life in every aspect, from his body to his voice.

"Phillip, good to see you," Thomas returned the greeting.

I noted with more than a little pride that Thomas seemed to match the other man in strength when they shook hands. *My man was no wimp.*

"What brings you to Paradise Point?" Phillip asked, scouring his counter for keys and paperwork.

"Just taking a break to get away. Thought I'd take Colby here to see everything your fine city has to offer."

Phillip finally looked up and noticed me. Not that I minded being completely ignored by an innkeeper or anything, but hey, I'm not invisible either.

I smiled and held out my hand. He stared at me and pointedly ignored my outstretched hand. I pulled it back slowly, as though I never offered it to him in the first place, pretending to stretch my arms.

I looked at Thomas and said brightly, "So far I'm lovin' the local hospitality."

"Thomas, you know you're always welcome but she"—he grunted while nodding in my direction—"can't stay here."

Thomas moved toward Phillip, leaning over the counter in a semimenacing sort of way, saying, "She goes where I go. You know the law now, Phillip. No discriminating."

"I'm not talking about discriminating. I'm talking about safety. I can't guarantee you won't be harassed here. You know Paradise Point considers itself outside of Tribunal law."

So Phillip was a bigot, but he was a *safety-conscious* bigot, so I guess that made everything okay. Not!

"No one is going to go up against a Tribunal Investigator, especially when he's accompanied by the Protector."

Phillip grunted and looked me over one more time. I tried to stand a little taller and look a bit more menacing. The way Thomas said my title, even I wanted to look behind me and see who he was talking about. It sounded downright impressive and a little intimidating. Too bad I was wearing a pink tank top, lacy shrug and black broomstick skirt with butterfly flip-flops. I hardly struck fear in the hearts of vampires anywhere.

"I just don't want any trouble," Phillip hedged but gave us keys to a room anyway.

"No trouble," Thomas promised. "You won't even know we're here."

We moved away but not before I caught the look of disgust on Phillip's face when he looked at me. This guy obviously thought Thomas and I were going to be spending all our time in the room, and he was revolted at the thought of intimacies with me. With *me*?! I might not be any Ileana Romanav but I was still one cute package. Jerk.

I shuffled behind Thomas down the hallway and ran into his back when he stopped to unlock the door.

"Oomph."

"Sorry," I mumbled, caught up in a tiny pity party for one. Sure, Phillip was a jerk and all but it wasn't like Thomas was all ready and willing to throw me down on the bed and ravage my half-blood self. Maybe I was revolting on some level to Thomas?

Thomas swung the door open and ushered me inside. The room was done up in grays and blues, lighthouse artwork over the queen-size bed and a small bathroom next to the closet. It was a snug room with no windows but when you're a vampire, you hardly require an ocean view.

I dropped down on the edge of the bed and put my purse down by my feet. There were no other chairs in the room. I looked around for a television but came up empty. This room was made for one thing and one thing only. I sighed heavily.

Thomas misinterpreted my sigh and said, "Don't worry about what Phillip said, Colby. We'll be fine. We'll hang out until sundown and go rescue the half-bloods."

He sank down next to me and put an arm around my shoulder in a supportive, nonsexual sort of way. I leaned my head on his shoulder and asked, "Thomas, how did he know I was a half-blood?"

When Thomas didn't immediately answer, I raised my head to look into his eyes. "Do I look so different from regular vampires? I don't think so. I mean, sure I have the freaky yellow eye thing going for me, but I'm wearing my colored contacts, so that can't be it. I am just as pasty as he was." I gasped a little at the thought that crossed my mind next, "Do I *smell*? Do half-bloods have a revolting kind of odor I'm not aware of?"

I started to sniff my hand, arm and wrist when Thomas grabbed me and started to laugh.

"Colby, you don't smell. Well, you do smell, but it isn't some revolting telltale scent." He leaned closer to me and put his nose to the nape of my neck and inhaled deeply.

"You smell like peaches and cream. Like summertime." I closed my eyes and swayed toward him a moment, but quickly strengthened my resolve.

"Then how could he tell?"

It was Thomas's time to sigh deeply as he straightened up. "Shake my hand," he instructed.

"What?"

"Come on. Put out your hand and offer it to shake."

I stared at him dumbly for a moment then extended my right hand to shake. Thomas took my hand and lifted it to my face, so my vampire license was clearly visible.

"He could tell I was a half-blood by my license? Does my ring look that much different than everyone else's?"

"Your license is white gold and has a different crest. See how the shape is a rectangle? Look at mine. It's a circle and the engraving is different. See?"

I compared our two rings. They were definitely dissimilar.

But still, I doubted Phillip could really decipher the difference from such a distance.

I looked doubtfully at Thomas, who finally conceded, "Also, your photo was circulated to all the safe houses so they knew you were to get special treatment."

"Yeah, I felt special too."

"By special treatment, I mean you are to be kept safe and out of the way of other, less gracious vampires. Phillip was simply concerned he couldn't offer you a secure room."

"Well, this just blows," I finally said after a moment of speculation. "Everyone hates me. I can't even go incognito anywhere. It's like I'm 'Colby, Undead Lord of the Lepers.'" I punctuated my statement with air quotes. I mean really, *air quotes*? How lame was I?

Thomas gently took my quoting fingers and clasped them in his. He looked me in the eyes and said softly, "I don't think you're a lord of the lepers at all."

I held his gaze shyly and whispered, "Really?"

He nodded, slowly moving his lips toward mine. "Really."

Then he was kissing me and I couldn't have cared less about Phillip, vampires or a colony of lepers. Thomas was kissing me. His mouth was sweet, strong and oh so yummy.

After a moment, I became almost painfully aware that we were making out on a very soft bed where no one would interrupt us, and we had hours to kill. What more could a girl ask for? This was it. The moment. The time for Thomas and me to take it to the next level, and I was so more than ready.

We'd been dating forever and he was finally going to make me his, in every sense of the word.

Abruptly, Thomas ended our passionate kissing and stood up.

Or he was going to make me very, very angry, in every sense of the word.

"We should review our game plan," he panted, reaching for his briefcase and maps he'd dumped on the floor earlier.

I was in shock by his rude departure and sat there with my mouth hanging open while he rummaged through his notes.

"What the hell was that all about?" I finally managed to utter.

Thomas didn't even look up at me when he replied, "Colby, we don't have time for this."

I looked around the room and then down at my watch. I shook it at him in an exaggerated attempt to reinforce my next point. "We've got nothing but time until sundown, Thomas."

"This isn't the time or place for . . ." Thomas tried to reason with me but I exploded.

"This isn't the time or place?! Are you crazy? We are in a no-tell motel, all alone with hours to kill in a room where the only furniture is a big bed—we don't even have a television! Dude, the time and place is never going to get any better than this!"

Okay, so I agree my voice went all screechy, to a level only dogs could hear, but I was *upset*. If girls could get blue balls,

I think I had a raging case and I was sick of the whole hot/cold thing.

"Colby, we haven't been dating all that long . . ."

"Eight months, Thomas!" I thought I heard a dog bark, "Eight long freakin' months and you haven't even tried for third base!"

"Colby—"

"Do you think I'm some sort of kid you have to protect from everything? Thomas, I'm not even a virgin. You don't have to worry about the whole 'first time' thing. You can thank Aidan Reynolds for those thrilling two minutes in the backseat of his father's Volvo. I'm a mature woman who wants to be intimate with her boyfriend."

"Mature woman?" Thomas struggled to keep his composure. "I should have known you were a mature woman with demands of getting past third base."

I sat back as though he'd slapped me. Ouch. Was that necessary? I may not be the most eloquent of debaters but that rebuttal seemed a bit low, and downright mean.

Thomas raked his hand through his hair in frustration. "Look, Colby, I'm sorry, I shouldn't—"

"Oh no." I threw my hand up in a stop motion. "Don't apologize. I get it. I'm some dumb kid who couldn't possibly understand the consequences of my actions. Thank goodness someone of your *advanced years* is here to guide me or I might never know the thrill of being chaste and virtuous."

I grabbed my handbag and stormed to the door.

"Where are you going?" he asked, clearly upset by the turn of events.

"I am taking my immature self outside for a walk, in the sunshine. Care to join me?" My voice dripped sarcasm.

He clenched his jaw and narrowed his eyes in response.

"No, then? Very well." I swept out of the room as regally as I could. I barely reached the front door before bursting into tears. I raced out of the gravel parking lot and headed in the general direction of the beach.

My flip-flops were not the best choice for a long walk along the beach, so I took them off and made my way to the water. It was around six thirty in the morning and not a soul was on the beach.

Cautiously, I dipped a toe into the surf and shivered. It wasn't freezing, but nor was it a pleasant lukewarm. I kicked the sand and walked aimlessly, occasionally picking up shells or tossing seaweed out of my way.

I had a lot of pent-up frustration to work out of my system. Maybe Thomas and I were just not compatible? I dug in my purse for my cell phone. I needed to talk to someone. I punched in Piper's speed dial number, ignoring how early it was in the morning. Piper would understand, I assured myself. After the first ring I felt a prickle of guilt. I got her voice mail and hung up, instead of leaving a message. She was not going to answer this early.

I plopped myself down on the sand, pulled my knees up and hugged myself. I was all alone. No Piper, no Thomas. No one but me. And frankly, I didn't consider myself the best of company lately. How was I going to lead Psi Phi House and keep them safe if I couldn't even manage my own life?

After a good two hours of self-doubt and pity, I decided it was time to take some action. I wasn't one to feel sorry for myself and I felt best when I was formulating a plan. I had drive and tenacity. So much so I started a half-blood revolution when I could have staked myself and called it a day.

Well, I wasn't a quitter and there was no way I was going to let two half-bloods stay in bonded servitude if I could help it. Thomas might not want me but that didn't make me any less of a Protector. They were my only concern right now. I would figure out Thomas after I completed my mission.

I made my way back to the safe house, surprised I managed to walk as far as I did. When I finally reached the house, I snuck into our room, hoping he would be asleep. The covers on the bed were a mess, as though he'd spent most of his time tossing and turning. I smiled at the thought.

Checking the time, I decided a nap sounded like a good idea. I could still get up way before Thomas and sneak out. I tiptoed over to his side of the bed and grabbed the keys to the car and his map of the beach house and put them in my purse. Then I kicked off my shoes and lay down on the bed, as far away from Thomas as I could without falling off. I closed my eyes and sleep took me fairly quickly.

It was around 6 P.M. when I awoke. I glanced at Thomas, who was still asleep. With any luck, I could have the girls freed and on the first flight back to Seattle before any vampire, or Thomas, had a clue. I scribbled a short note explaining my task and informing Thomas that I would meet him back home.

Once outside our room, I hurried to the car, afraid I would be spotted by some vacationing Undead. Not that they knew who I was or even cared why I was there, as I doubted the Tribunal sent out an APB to every vampire in California, but still, my half-blood status was enough to raise the hackles of most vampires. No need to go flaunting myself in their favorite vacation destination.

Once I was safe outside the house I relaxed. I knew Cookie's place was less than a mile away and I had Thomas's map. It took no more than five minutes to arrive, despite taking a wrong turn. Twice. Hey, I never claimed to be a navigation expert, did I?

I double-checked the address, uncertain if the innocuous-looking home before me really housed vampires and half-blood slaves. It looked like any other beach house with its inviting wraparound porch that allowed for direct beach access. The house's whitewashed wood and its faded blue shutters had a welcoming quality that seemed downright homey.

Cautiously I approached the house from the beach access. I was surprised to see numerous college coeds sporting the latest beachwear. They were laughing and barbecuing. Something was not right here. I debated leaving and waiting for Thomas, but quickly shrugged off that idea. Surely I could handle this.

"Hi," one of the masses said to me.

"Come on up and join the party," another added.

Wow, an invitation to snoop around. What more could I ask for?

"Hi," I answered, "My name's, uh . . ." *Do I give my real name or do I give a fake name?* Seconds ticked by and I finally blurted out, "Brittany." Okay fine, so I panicked and they were playing "Toxic" on the radio. Sue me.

"Want a burger, Brittany?" a rather hunky blond in cargo shorts inquired.

"Thanks, but I'm good. Do you live here?" I asked him.

"Nah, this is Cookie's place. But everyone hangs out here. See those chicks over there?" I looked in the direction he pointed.

"Yeah."

"That's Tina and the dark-haired girl is Sage. They live here too."

"Wow, seems like quite a party house," I answered absently, staring at the two teens in question. These were my half-bloods and they were far from chained in a cellar. They were laughing and enjoying the summer rays, with no vampires in sight to keep them in line. What was really going on here?

"I think I'll go say hi," I said and wandered off in their direction. I was offered beer in a Solo cup on my way across the porch and pretended to take a sip. Ugh, not very cold, but I wasn't much of a beer fan anyway.

I reached the dark-haired gal named Sage first.

"Hi, Sage," I started the conversation as though we already

knew each other. I was betting on the fact that she met so many people she wouldn't remember if she knew me or not.

"Oh hi," she said brightly, confirming my suspicion that she was going to pretend she knew me because I said her name.

"I see Tina. Is Cookie around?" If I was going to pretend I knew her, I might as well go whole hog and pretend to know the entire household.

"Oh, you know Cookie? She's such a night owl." Sage laughed, tossing her hair back over her shoulder.

I took a gamble and said, "Yeah, vampires are like that."

She stepped backward and glanced around her nervously. "That's funny. Night person, vampire. Ha ha."

"Yeah, I'm a laugh riot." I stared at her a moment before continuing. "Listen, Sage, I'm here to rescue you."

She looked confused. "Rescue me? What do you mean?"

I sighed deeply and explained, "I'm here to take you and Tina back to Psi Phi House. I'm the Protector."

If anything, she looked more confused than ever.

"I don't know anything about a Psi Phi House or any Protector. Besides, why would I want to do that? This is my home."

"But you're a prisoner here," I argued. She obviously didn't know anything about me or the changes in the law. Were they drugging these girls?

"Hardly." She snorted. "Cookie takes care of us. I get to party all the time and hang out with friends. If that's a prison, lock me up and throw away the key." She giggled a bit at her own joke.

I counted to ten in my head to keep from throttling her. She should be weeping with relief and thanking me profusely for taking her away from vampire suppression. Instead she was whining about how much fun she would be leaving behind.

"Do you get to come and go as you please?" I asked.

"Well, no. Cookie wants to make sure we're safe so she has someone escort us around town. You know how vampires feel about half-bloods." She leaned forward and whispered the last sentence in a confidential tone.

Boy, did I ever.

"So, you get to party all the time and hang with friends. Sounds like a pretty good deal. She lets you do that out of the goodness of her own heart or do you have some sort of arrangement going? Like you two do all the housework in exchange for living here?"

She visibly relaxed once I stopped hounding her to leave and wanted to know how she hooked up with such a sweet deal. Don't get me wrong, they were still coming with me, but I needed to know the scoop before I could get them to see things my way.

"Well, I guess the arrangement is more like we're hostesses. We keep the party going until late in the evening, when Cookie has her, uh, guests over." She looked a tad uncomfortable at this revelation.

"Oh, I get it. You party up the tourists until they pass out all over the house. Then Cookie's vampire posse comes over and gets to pick and choose over a smorgasbord of coeds, sort of buffet-style."

Sage brightened immediately. "Yes, that's it exactly. It's a win-win situation."

Unless you're the buffet.

"So what happens if something gets out of control? Like someone drinks too much . . . vamp or partygoer? Has that happened before?"

Sage looked away a moment before answering. "Sure, it's happened, but for the most part things are cool."

I nodded in understanding. Of course it's happened. And judging by the way Sage was acting, all guilt-ridden, I had the feeling it happened a little more often than she was letting on.

"What are you again?" she wondered aloud.

"I'm the Protector. I'm a half-blood too."

She shook her head as though in denial. "No, you can't be."

"Well, I'm certainly not a vampire." I smiled at her while indicating the sun. "And you're welcome to take my pulse if you want to check and see if I'm alive." I offered her my pale extremity for examination.

She shook her head, apparently deciding I was telling the truth. "What does a Protector do?"

"I guess you could say that it's my job to make sure you get to live as you want to. Psi Phi House is a place half-bloods go to learn about the vampire world and get acclimated to their role as a free Undead. I protect all half-bloods from harm. So what happens tomorrow, Sage?" I asked her.

"What do you mean?"

"Well, is it a party every day or do you get to do anything

to shake up the monotony? The beach life is great and all but don't you get a little bored after a while?"

"Well, sure. When the beach scene slows down, then we hit the town and see if we can drum up some action to bring back to the house."

"Sounds like a lot of work for a place to stay," I commented while looking around the porch. Still pretty light on the party-goers.

"What do you mean?" she asked.

Aha, I had her interested now. Step into my parlor said the spider to the fly.

"I'm just saying you work pretty hard for Cookie and all you're getting is a roof over your head and meals, so to speak. Tomorrow brings the same old thing. Don't you want more out of life?"

She stared at me for a moment before saying, very softly, "I'm dead."

"Ah, now there's where you are wrong, Sage. You're Un-dead. And with the recent law changes at the Tribunal, half-bloods have the same rights as vampires. Meaning you can live out your Undead existence in peace, not hiding from the Investigators or doing the bidding of another vampire, no mat-ter how nice," I interjected quickly when she started to ob-ject. "You could have a second chance.

"I bet Cookie is a great gal, but you didn't ask to be turned, did you? Of course not. Don't you want to go to college? Get a job doing something that interests you and challenges your mind? I'm all for a good party once in a while but really, aren't you getting a little bored?"

She looked down at her pink toenails and nodded.

I was on a roll. With any luck, I would have the girls packed and ready to grab the first flight back to Seattle before sunset. *Take that, Thomas,* I thought smugly.

"Why don't you call Tina over here and we can talk a little about Psi Phi House and the new laws. Just so you have a clear understanding of all your options." She agreed and waved Tina over.

Honestly, at this point I was feeling a bit like an evangelist. I answered their questions and explained the new laws, in layman's terms. Both girls were absolutely stunning but not the sharpest pencils in the box. They were more concerned with how many parties the sorority would have and the male to female ratio of the college than about assimilation into Vampire society.

Despite her nefarious reasons, in a way, I was grateful Cookie had taken them under her wing. They could have come to a much less appealing existence if the wrong type of vampire found them.

All in all it took less than an hour to convince Tina and Sage to pack up and leave with me on the next flight. I left the Tribunal's paperwork on the refrigerator so Cookie would eventually find it but it wouldn't be the first thing she saw. No use tempting fate and risking a confrontation.

Tina was easier to convince with Sage already on board

with the idea. She mentioned it would be a good time since she just broke up with her boyfriend and he wasn't taking it very well. I was a humanitarian on all levels and couldn't wait to get back to Seattle. Sure, Thomas would be a bit pissed that I'd completed the mission without him—and with such stellar success—but he'd get over it.

I helped load up the car with their luggage. I suggested leaving behind the unnecessary stuff. After all, the beach house was still their home, technically. No reason to get them completely freaked out by saying they could never come back again.

By the time we reached the airport, I had a tiny pinprick of pain throbbing behind my left eye. A sure sign a migraine was coming on. You'd think being Undead would spare me from such things, but two hours in a car with Sage and Tina apparently superseded the dead/Undead boundaries of a common headache.

Tina lamented her failed relationship with Lance contemplated reestablishing her previous vegan lifestyle.

"Don't you think that may be a bit difficult?" I questioned.

"You're the one who told me I could live my existence the way I wanted to. That I didn't have to do what other vampires told me," she argued.

"But Tina, if you don't drink blood, you'll die. That's kind of the requisite of being a vampire, half-blood or not."

"But I don't want to live off of animal by-products," she wailed to no one in particular. "It's against everything I believe in."

Tina patted her shoulder reassuringly and I bit my tongue

to keep from saying some pretty unflattering things about her flawed thinking. It was one thing to be a vegan as a living human but living off of blood was a vampire's only option. She couldn't just suck carrot juice and go about her life doing the happy dance.

This was just one of many conversations we had and by the time we touched down at Sea-Tac, I had a headache the size of Washington State. Gone was my illusion of a plane ride filled with polite conversation. No one asked me questions about Psi Phi House and or the new laws. I expected a certain reserve between total strangers, you know what I mean? But no. Apparently, Sage and Tina's lives were an open book. And an open audiobook at that.

Tina filled me in on the details of her tragic breakup with Lance, a vampire surfer no less. "I mean, did he really think I was going to hang out on the beach all night and watch him surf? Hello?! Like I don't have a life of my own or something?"

They sat on either side of me. Tina regaling me with Lance's selfishness and Sage parroting everything Tina said back to me. "He thinks he is so cool because he surfs at night," Tina would say and then Sage would interject, "He totally does."

I was beginning to think that Cookie had hoodwinked the entire Tribunal by holding out and keeping these two until we came in and took them by force. Thereby ridding herself of the chatty half-bloods forever. All without having to lift a finger. In my mind, Cookie was a friggin' mastermind genius and I was her duped patsy.

I called Piper as soon as we landed to get a ride but she icily reminded me she was shopping with the others and was unavailable to jump up and do my bidding. Ouch. Piper pissed was not something I wanted to deal with right now. Instead, I called up my dad and he picked us up. We loaded up Mom's Jag (I have no idea how he managed to talk her into *that*) with all their belongings, which included a rather large stuffed unicorn collection. (I paid fifty bucks for an extra bag so Tina could keep all the fluffy babies Lance had given her, ugh!)

Dad seemed pretty disappointed that both Tina and Sage not only had lovely smiles, but fully functioning fangs as well. I guess when you're the only orthodontist in town who specialized in fang headgear, it's a bit disappointing when no one needs your services.

"I'm so thirsty," Sage announced after her stomach growled. I didn't care for the way she was eyeing my dad's neck so I suggested he take us to Dick's Burgers. Dick's had been around forever in Seattle and was always hopping. Especially late at night. I was surprised when Sage ordered a chocolate milk shake.

"You can keep that down?" I asked in awe.

"Oh sure. Tina can't do the milk thing, but I can."

Neither could I.

"Okay, so how much time do you need?"

"I can take this in the car. We don't have to wait on me."

She started to saunter back toward my dad, all eyes in the order line watched her every move. Sage was pretty riveting, especially sipping her shake through a straw.

"Don't you need to . . ." I nodded toward the crowd. "You know, feed?"

She waved her hand in dismissal. "Oh, gosh no. I've been grazing all day. I really just wanted something to drink."

I shook my head in exasperation. Tina finally joined us after getting the key to a restroom.

"I just met the nicest guy. He let me feed, right there by his car. So nice of him," she gushed and waved to a dark-haired fellow standing next to a white Jeep. He looked a bit pale and dazed but otherwise returned her wave with enthusiasm.

"Are all guys in Seattle so nice?" she continued to chatter, making my dad squirm in his seat after we all got back into the car.

"Well, that depends on what you mean by nice. Do all guys offer to open a vein and let you feed in the parking lot of Dick's? Then I would have to say no. You must have found the exception to the rule."

She bounced lightly in the backseat, looking out the window and taking in the scenery. "He was just so nice," she said again and I exchanged a look with my dad. I suspected her "nice" guy had been on something by the way she was suddenly so wired and chatty.

It was one thing to teach the value of clean living but as a vampire, we could only keep our living as clean as the blood we drank. If our meals were high as a kite, then . . .

There just hadn't been time for Tina to make sure she was getting clean blood. Now she was loopy. I just hoped her friendly Seattle conquest wasn't strung out on Ecstasy, because then things would get very interesting at Psi Phi House.

We arrived in record time. My dad practically threw the luggage out of the trunk.

"Thanks, Dad. I really appreciate your help. Want to come inside for some coffee?" I offered, not wanting him to drive home if he was tired.

"No, dear." He kissed my forehead and moved back toward the driver's side of the car. "I have an early morning tomorrow. Mom and I will stop by and see how you are doing this weekend. Maybe bring out Aunt Chloe."

I waved to him and he was off. I looked back at Tina, who was staring up at the sky and softly singing "Twinkle, Twinkle Little Star," and Sage, who had removed her sandals and was walking across the front lawn, feeling the dew between her toes. No wonder he opted for escape. *I* wanted to escape. Smart man.

I loaded myself up with their luggage and entered the house. After two more trips, I had all of their stuff in the foyer. I showed the girls to an upstairs bedroom and then explained how they would sleep downstairs. Though Sage and Tina could handle the sun without instant spontaneous combustion, it was easier to have everyone sleeping in the basement behind the secret door. Not that Ileana or her maid cared about my concern for their health. The extra privacy interested them more.

I left them upstairs, putting away their clothes. I noted the only things they seemed to own were shorts, scanty tops and bikinis. It was going to be a mite chilly for them come fall. No one else was home and I wandered around aimlessly, peeking into Ileana's bedroom to see how much progress she'd made in unpacking. It looked like a totally different room!

She'd moved some of the furniture out, I noted, to make room for her more personal items. Shaking my head, I shut the door. I chose not to deal with her rule-breaking at that moment. I was going to live in denial until I had a better idea of what I wanted to do.

I wandered back downstairs and sank into the fluffy couch in our living room and debated calling Thomas. It did not escape my attention that he hadn't called my cell phone to yell at me for deserting him, so he must be very angry indeed. I decided to wait on that confrontation as well. I was one big mass of avoidance. That is, until I heard a car pull up to the house.

I rolled off the couch and peeked outside. A small transit van stopped by the sidewalk and my fellow sorority sisters emerged, laden down with bags upon bags of Nordstrom goodies. Lucy was laughing at something Ileana said, while Sophie, Ileana's maid, struggled with several shoe boxes.

I bit my tongue in annoyance. Ileana hardly needed the Tribunal to buy her new clothes, but I was happy to see Lucy and Angie seemed to have a nice collection of packages. I noticed Carl had joined them, looking bored and stressed at the same time. *How does one do such a thing?* I wondered.

Piper jumped out with a single bag that I suspected held a pair of boots. Piper loved boots. I opened the door to welcome them home.

"Hey all!" I called from the door. Everyone looked up and a few called out a similar greeting. I hopped down the steps and offered my carrying services. Piper loaded me up with bags from the back of the van. *Wow, they really went to town,* I thought, after my second trip from the van to the house.

Once inside, all the girls carried their plunder upstairs to their rooms. I told them I would be up in a moment to see what they got and explained we had two new house sisters upstairs. Once they were out of ear shot, I asked Piper how things went.

She took my arm, steered me toward the back of the house into the housemother's bedroom, now filled to the brim with Ileana's packing trunks, and sat me down on the bed.

This did not bode well.

"That bad?" I guessed, watching her pace three feet either way, back and forth next to the bed.

She stopped a moment and looked me in the eye. "Should I start with the shoplifting or the threats to put a cap in Mrs. Durham's ass?"

"Oh my," was all I could say.

"We arrived promptly at closing time and met Durham at the concierge desk. After a very long and patronizing speech about the generosity of the Tribunal and the grace of vampires everywhere letting half-bloods exist, she told everyone to pick out exactly two things and meet back at the cash register."

I started to interrupt but Piper waved me quiet.

"Well, I was hardly going to let her get away with that so I amended her statement and told the girls to pick out whatever they wanted, but they only had an hour to shop. They immediately split but Durham was pissed at me. I assured her that no one could possibly do too much damage in only an hour and she relented. Not at all gracefully, I might add.

"Anyway, she wandered off to get her own stuff and I wanted to pick up a pair of boots I noticed when we arrived. Then I started to hear a commotion across in cosmetics."

I nodded at her, caught up in the story.

"I hurried over to the MAC counter, where Durham and Angie are *screaming* at each other—I thought they were about to duke it out, right there in front of the lipstick case. It seems Durham didn't think cosmetics should be included in the shopping spree and Angie, who apparently is very fond of makeup, told her it should be included as part of a wardrobe because who would consider themselves completely dressed without lipstick?

"Anyway, Durham suggests to Angie, who just helped herself to the testers, that she looks like a streetwalker and she was doing her a favor by limiting her makeup accessibility."

"Oh no," I gasped.

"Oh yes," Piper confirmed. "So, Lucy said there was no reason to get personal and Durham tells Lucy to shut up, which makes Angie call Durham a bleepin' cow."

I winced because I knew Piper was replacing more colorful vocabulary with "bleeping." She noticed the look on my face and assured me, "Oh, it gets better."

I was afraid of that.

"So I say let's all calm down and Angie proclaims that she refuses to be in debt to a bleepin' cow and therefore won't be buying a thing. At the same time she started taking the clothes in her hand and shoving them under her shirt and in her sweatpants. Like she's just gonna walk on out of Nordstrom laden down with stolen goods and no one will dare stop her."

In spite of the seriousness of the story, I started to giggle.

"I told everyone to continue shopping, since they don't have much time left, and took Angie aside. I assured her that she could have whatever makeup she wants and I would be happy to 'buy' the clothes she has stuffed under her shirt so she won't be indebted to Durham. After a few minutes, Angie agreed but not before announcing, very loudly, that if Mrs. Durham gets in her way again she's gonna put a cap in her ass."

"Piper, I don't know what to say. How awful." And in truth it did sound awful. But I couldn't stop the giggles from escaping. I could easily picture Piper playing diplomat, all the while cursing me under her breath and trying to keep everyone from going postal.

"Don't you dare laugh," she warned me, but she was having a hard time keeping herself from giggling as well. Finally, she couldn't contain her mirth any longer and we both laughed until we cried. She joined me on the bed, wiping the tears and smeared eyeliner off her cheeks.

"I am so sorry you had to go through that. I know Durham can be a pain, but I had no idea she would take it out on everyone. I figured she would wait until she saw me again."

"Yeah, well, you thought wrong. How did it go in California?"

"I brought home the two half-bloods with no bloodshed if that's what you mean."

"Where's Thomas?" she asked.

"He stayed behind. He's going to talk to Cookie about the half-bloods and then head home."

This technically wasn't a lie because he would go to the beach house when it was dark and discover I'd really taken the girls and he would have to deal with the wrath of Cookie.

"Hmmmm," she said, staring at me speculatively.

"And we kind of had a fight," I admitted.

"I see. What kind of fight?"

"Oh Piper, it was awful," I wailed. "We were making out in our room on this huge bed and he just stands up and is all 'We've got to figure out a game plan' and I'm all 'What? We've got hours to kill before sunset' and he's 'This isn't the time or the place' and I'm all, 'Dude, this is totally the time and place' and then"—I took a deep breath and wailed again—"then he called me immature!" I hiccupped dramatically for effect, waiting for Piper to console me.

"You tried to seduce him when you two were at work?" she asked, incredulously.

"Of course not. We weren't at work *at that moment*. We were waiting. We had hours of waiting to do. And the mean guy at the reception desk was acting all icky toward me, saying I couldn't stay and all. Just because I'm a half-blood." Again I ended my tirade with a slight wail, waiting for Piper to agree with me.

"But you know vampires don't like half-bloods," she tried to reason with me.

"Piper!" I said in exasperation. "The point is that I was vulnerable and needed comfort from my boyfriend and he wouldn't *put out*."

"But he's never put out. Why would that moment make things any different?"

"Aarghh. We had a private room, a big bed, no one to disturb us and hours to kill with no TV."

"Oh, you didn't have a television? Well, I guess that does change things a little bit."

Sometimes I just wanted to bite Piper . . . really hard. But I refrained because she sounded like she was finally coming around.

"So out of the blue Thomas says you're immature and that's why he won't do you?" I could tell Piper was struggling to understand but since she wasn't there it was very hard for her to grasp the facts. The facts were I was totally right and Thomas was cruel and insensitive.

"Well, not really. I told him I wasn't a virgin so what was the big deal anyway?"

Piper gave me a pained expression.

"Ouch," she said.

"Yes, exactly. That's what I thought."

"I meant ouch for Thomas. That must have been nice to hear."

"What do you mean?"

"Oh, I don't know. He's an old-fashioned guy and is being

totally respectful by waiting on the physical side of things. He's training you and helping you to become a better Protector. He's dating a half-blood, so I imagine he's being ostracized by all the other vampires and his girlfriend screams she isn't a virgin *in his face* when he won't put out because he's concerned about a mission to protect half-bloods, which is her responsibility in the first place. So yeah, I stand behind my 'ouch.'"

I looked at Piper, somewhat dazed. Well, yeah, when you put it that way.

"Crap," I whispered, dragging my hands through my hair.

Five

Piper left me with my shame. I guess she sensed it was time to let her logic sink in. I lay down on the bed, debating if I should grab a little sleep. I was used to sleeping only a couple of hours at a time. In order to graduate from high school, I had to be able to attend my day classes, so I learned to survive off of napping. Instead I decided to search out my sorority sisters. After all, they were my job. I was in the business of protecting them. It seemed natural to assume they might eke out a little gratitude and I could desperately use a pick-me-up.

I wandered upstairs and found Ileana going through her new purchases. She was giving orders to her maid to hang this, press that and put away the other. When she was satisfied everything would be accomplished to her satisfaction, she brushed past me and headed downstairs.

"Doesn't it bother you?" I asked the maid from the doorway, fed up with "Sophie, fetch this for me."

"No mum," she answered quietly, never tarrying from her task.

"Well for heaven's sake, why not? You're a human being and deserve to be treated with respect. Don't you want more out of life than jumping up to do *her*"—I gestured my thumb in Ileana's direction—"bidding?"

"My family has been in the service of the Romanavs for centuries. It is an honor to serve my lady."

"Really?" I puzzled, wondering if a long-standing employee/employer relationship was really worth putting up with Ileana.

"Yes, my lady has been very good to my family."

"Oh, do you have brothers and sisters who work for her as well?" I leaned against the door frame.

"No mum, I am an only child. Every daughter serves my lady. I do, and my mother, and her mother before her. It has always been so."

"Wow, so your mom and grandma served Ileana's mom and her grandmother?" Talk about a family business.

Sophie stopped her folding actions and looked at me in speculation, then turned back to her task. "As I said, my family has served the Romanavs for centuries."

Well, okay then. I left her to her lady's maid tasks and went in search of Carl.

Carl and I began our relationship hating each other. Back when I was first changed, he thought I was mocking him when he asked to see my fangs and I showed him my stainless steel fang headgear. But over the last eight months, we'd become almost friends. Actually, I think he still had a thing for Piper but she hadn't shown any romantic interest in him after he was her date for Homecoming. She liked him well enough but wasn't willing to date a vampire, and I couldn't blame her. Relationships were tough enough without adding the whole Undead thing into the mix. I worked with Carl and over time, I managed to grow on him. Much like a fungus, he was fond of saying.

I figured he wouldn't be too thrilled to hear how I left Thomas stuck in California. When I found Carl at the massive dining room table, poring over some paperwork from his briefcase, he smirked as I entered the room and commented, "Never a dull moment around you, is there?"

"Ah, I see Thomas has filled you in." I grabbed the chair across from him and sank into it.

"Breaking rank and leaving your partner essentially locked in a safe house while you placed yourself in danger is grounds for an inquiry."

"I did not lock anyone in a safe house!" I hotly refuted. "I left him asleep in his room in the middle of the day! It's not my fault he can't go out in the sun. And, for your information, I am the Protector of the half-bloods and I shouldn't have to wait for an Investigator to go talk to them."

Carl raised an eyebrow and replied, "Thomas is not any Investigator, he was the one assigned to you on this case *and* he's your senior."

Before I could reply, a new voice added itself to the conversation.

"And by ditching him and playing Wonder Vamp, you kind of rolled his face in the fact that you didn't need him there and that he has no value. No value as an Investigator or as your boyfriend. Nice job."

I turned to glare at Piper. "I did *not* devalue my boyfriend. He knows how much I, uh, I value him." Who uses "value" in a sentence that doesn't include "shopping," anyway? Not value Thomas? Sheesh, how could Piper say these things to me after I shared my pain with her?

"I'm just saying . . ."

"Well, don't," I said, cutting her off rudely. "Thomas and I are fine. He'll be just fine. You just don't get it. Our relationship is complex," I added a little lamely, feeling myself sink into a shame spiral. Thomas was always doing whatever he could to help me and I had kind of slapped him down on this one. I shouldn't have let my anger about our personal situation affect my job.

It's just he made me so mad, acting like he knew everything and I was a newbie loser who couldn't even walk on the beach in the middle of the day without wreaking havoc. Well, I did just fine. And my success would be just the eye-opener he needed to see I could take care of myself.

Piper threw her hands up and muttered, "Whatever," and walked back into the living room. I stood up and glared at Carl, daring him to contradict me. He turned back to his paperwork, effectively dismissing me.

Well excuse me for living, er, *not living*.

I stomped away in a bit of a huff. Didn't anybody see my side of this? I was doing the best I could do at this stupid job. A job which I never asked for, by the way, and no one seemed to appreciate how hard I'd been working at it. Not Piper, not Carl and especially not Thomas.

I climbed the stairs to my bedroom and threw myself on the bed. I lay on my back, looking up at the ceiling, hugging my fluffy pink throw pillow to my chest. *Would it ever get any easier?* I thought and then my stomach growled. I groaned at the injustice.

Just then a timid knock interrupted my pity party (I *hate* that) and my door cracked open to reveal Lucy.

"Hey," she said.

"Hey," I returned her greeting.

"If you have time, do you, uh, want to see what we picked out shopping?" she asked shyly.

Ah yes, the infamous shopping trip to Nordstrom. The event that would forever leave me in Piper's debt.

I hemmed a bit. "Well, actually . . ."

Lucy rushed to add, "And I hoped you could go with me to feed? You know, show me where . . ." She paused with a hopeful look on her face.

What kind of ogre was I, anyway? Poor thing just wanted some company and to eat, but was too timid to go alone and I'm all "poor me." I sucked as a Protector.

"I was actually going to suggest feeding. Great minds think

alike, I guess. We'll see who else wants to come with us. Then you could show me your stuff, if you're still up for it?"

Lucy blinked twice and said, "Sure, great. Let's do that."

I smiled at her enthusiasm. Maybe everything wasn't a complete disaster. I could make some friends out of this gig and maybe, just maybe things would turn out okay.

"Great, let me grab my fangs and we can go." I reached for my nightstand and pulled out the familiar box which housed my headgear fangs.

"I'm sorry, I thought you said you had to get your fangs." Lucy giggled at the thought.

"Well, actually I did. I don't have real fangs." I was embarrassed each time I had to explain my lack of canines to another vampire. It wasn't my fault I had six teeth removed for braces when I was twelve. My orthodontist (also known as Dad's best friend, Ted) suggested oral surgery to remove my wisdom teeth and two canines. Unfortunately, though I now had a killer smile, I no longer had my feeding fangs.

So my dad, a gifted orthodontist in his own right, created special headgear with stainless-steel fangs so I could still feed. Yes, it made me look like the biggest geek in the vampire world but at least I didn't starve. Which normally seemed like a pretty good trade-off until I had to explain why I had to wear the headgear. Like now.

I showed them to Lucy, who wanted to see what they looked like on. I slipped them into place and she carefully examined how they fit, the sharpness of the fangs and its overall effectiveness. She didn't laugh at me and nodded in support.

"Ingenious," she announced. "You're very lucky your father would make these for you." She sounded so solemn I asked about her family.

"I have no one," she answered, then quickly changed the subject.

In the end we picked up Angie and surprise, surprise, Ileana to make the feeding rounds. Sage and Tina were worn out and not at all hungry. They decided to kick back and watch reruns of *The Simpsons* and veg out downstairs.

Instead of driving we opted to walk to the nearest park by the university. There were bound to be dozens of students or teens hanging around, bent on misdemeanors.

After I informed Carl where we were going (to which he just grunted in response—men are so touchy) we headed out the door, where I found Piper getting into her car.

"Hey," I said, noting she was leaving without saying good-bye.

"Hey," she responded, looking a little guilty at being caught sneaking out.

"We are headed out to fee—er, get some fresh air," I finished lamely. Sometimes it was really hard having a best friend who wasn't Undead. The Living were kind of squeamish about the whole feeding thing.

"Cool, I'm just on my way home. Gotta get some sleep and all before we have to catch our flight."

My mouth fell open as I remembered that Piper was leaving

tomorrow, er, today since it was after midnight. She would be gone for ten whole days in England with her mom.

She took one look at my face and retorted, hands on hips, "You *do* remember I'm leaving for England, right?"

The problem was, I hadn't remembered she was leaving. I mean, I knew she was leaving but with having to go pick up Sage and Tina, then leaving Thomas in California, I completely lost track of time. Instead of pouting about my circumstances, I should have been spending the evening with Piper before she left the country. It was official. I was the world's worst best friend.

"Of course I remembered." I decided to take the wounded friend role, since I wasn't about to admit I'd lost track of the days. "I just thought you wouldn't leave without saying goodbye first."

Ha, dodge that one, Little Missy.

Piper, of course, was way too smart to play my game, which is one of the reasons she is my best friend. She doesn't put up with my crap. A blessing and curse, I can assure you.

"Dude . . ." She drew out the word and tilted her head to the side as though she couldn't believe I would even try the wounded friend thing on her.

I walked over to her car, leaving the other vamps clumped together in an awkward circle, trying to pretend they couldn't hear every word of our conversation.

"Piper, I didn't forget you were going out of town," I tried to reassure her but had to add, "I just . . . didn't remember you were leaving so soon."

Whereas I didn't want to hurt Piper's feelings by admitting I forgot, she had no such problem with me.

"You suck," she said pointedly.

Ugh.

"I know, I know. It's all part of the insensitive vampire package. I'm sorry, Piper, I really am. I, I just didn't want to think about you not being around, is all."

My voice broke toward the end of this dark confession. I didn't want to think of Piper leaving me alone with all my Protector responsibilities. She'd been by my side since I turned Undead and I wasn't sure I could do it all alone. Really alone, since I was sure to have pissed off Thomas with my freedom flight out of California.

Piper put her fingers on my lips and mocked, "Stop. You had me at insensitive."

Man, with friends like these, who needed enemies?

She dropped her fingers away and I laughed. So we would be okay. I moved forward and gave her a quick hug.

"I'll e-mail you every day you're gone," I promised.

She returned my hug quickly then pushed away. "Sheesh, not every day. I do have a life you know. I plan to be sightseeing and stuff." But she smiled when she said it so I knew she would be looking forward to hearing from me.

"Be safe," I reminded her as she opened her car door.

"Always," she assured me haughtily and climbed into her car. Then she was gone. My stomach growled insistently and I turned back to my group of charges, shuffling uncomfortably on the front lawn.

"Oh, for heaven's sake, are we going to feed or not?" Ileana demanded.

I sighed deeply and motioned for the group to follow me. I was missing Piper already. We walked west for several blocks to a rather large park just south of the university campus. There were several open-all-night food places and the park always seemed to be brimming with activity. Tonight was no exception, and I suspected we would easily be able to feed without drawing any undue attention to ourselves.

"Okay, why don't we split up and make the rounds?" I suggested.

"Do we meet back here when we're done?" asked Lucy. I hadn't planned on all of us rendezvousing after we were done, but the look on Lucy's face made me realize that the others weren't as confident on their own as I was. Actually, none of them were even from Seattle, no wonder they looked like lost little sheep.

"Sure, if everyone is cool with that?" I glanced around at the group and they seemed to be in agreement. "Shall we say one hour from now?" Again more nodding from the group.

I turned to walk into the park, on a trail that took me through a heavily treed area and noticed all the girls still standing in a group, looking around the area but not moving a muscle. I stopped and asked, "Everything okay?"

"Where should we go?" Angie asked.

"Um, anywhere. You could try near the Taco Bell or over there next to those cars parked by the video store or . . ." They were each staring blankly at me. Oh, for heaven's sake.

"Why don't you all come with me?" I suggested instead and they immediately jumped to join me. We took a leisurely stroll through the park and into the shading trees.

"What I find that works is just to hang out until someone walks by. Then I ask them to come over and stand still, I feed and send them on their merry way."

"Where's the fun in that?" Ileana snorted.

"What do you mean, fun? It's feeding. It's not supposed to be fun," I retorted, irritated by her attitude.

"We are predators by our very design. Waiting in the path for some unsuspecting person to walk by hardly seems very sporting." It was almost pleasant to hear Ileana talk, with her soft rolling accent—if you didn't listen to the actual words coming out of her mouth.

"How do you feed at home, Ileana?" Lucy asked.

"Well, I have Sophie bring me my meals, of course. I don't go traipsing around a park." She turned up her pert little nose and looked around her surroundings.

"Predators hide in the brush and wait for their prey. I see it all the time on the Discovery Channel," Sage offered to the group. I felt a pinprick of pain start behind my left eye. Not enough to really hurt, just enough to irritate me. Much like the group was beginning to do. Looked like my migraine was coming back in full force.

"Predators kill to survive. May I remind you that none of us needs to kill to do that? We take what we need and that's all."

"Well, no one needs to eat more than one slice of cake but

we've all been known to gorge once in a while." Ileana giggled at her little joke and I rounded to face her.

I kept my tone even, eyes level with hers, and explained slowly, "No one in Psi Phi House gorges. Understand?"

Everyone else nodded vigorously but Ileana simply sighed. "Whatever. My, you really are touchy, aren't you?"

I was ready to argue some more when the breeze changed and I caught an unfamiliar scent. I shoved Ileana to the side sharply and leapt past her in one swift motion. I landed in time to block the stake that came within an inch of embedding itself in her back. My surprise attacker was wearing black (so cliché) and his fangs were bared.

The girls screamed in surprise but I was already countering his next move. He was strong, but then so was I. He struck quickly on the offensive and it took all my concentration to keep from getting impaled. I wouldn't last long in this fight if I didn't think of something quick. He lunged toward me again and this time I took his arm and pulled forward, sidestepping the stake. The momentum of our combined energy threw him off balance long enough for me to kick at the back of his knee and down he went.

A quick clip to the side of his temple with my foot rendered him momentarily stunned. I dropped down onto his back and wretched the stake from his hand. I'd hoped to knock the air from his lungs, but being a vampire and all, there wasn't a lot of air occupying his lungs.

I wasn't sure what to do next. I wanted to know more

about him but I could hardly keep a vampire subdued without keeping him unconscious. And I hardly felt like carrying his body back to the house.

Just then another vampire made his presence known by grabbing Angie from behind. I quickly struck my hostage unconscious and leapt up to help her. I looked to the other girls. Where was Lucy? Ileana seemed to snap out of her daze when Angie was grabbed. She reached into her bag and pulled out, could it be? A Taser.

Ileana pointed it at Angie's attacker and fired. The vampire released Angie, but stood frozen, shaking as who knows how many volts of electricity surged through his body. Angie fell, somewhat stunned; she must have absorbed some of the Taser's voltage.

"Ileana!" I yelled at her. "That's not going to stop a vampire."

I was right but it sure did slow him down. I took both my fists and clapped them together at his temples, knocking him out. With the exception of not being in the black zone and taken by surprise, I think Cyrus would have been proud by the way I took out two vampire assailants. Well, okay, one vampire assailant. Ileana seemed to be doing okay without me.

I checked around quickly to make sure there were no more. Lucy appeared, as if out of nowhere, at Angie's side and announced she would be fine in a moment. Ileana efficently unclamped her victim and put the Taser back in her purse, calm as you please.

"What in the world are you doing carrying a stun gun?" I demanded. Ileana simply shrugged in response.

"Who are they?" Angie asked, trying to shake off her shock.

"My guess is vampires who don't care for half-bloods," responded Ileana coolly.

"We should get out of here," Lucy suggested, looking around nervously. Lucy might outlive us all because her fight-or-flight instinct seemed to be heavy on the flight, not so much fight.

I tried to concur but my stomach growled again, drowning out my agreement. Slowly, a smile spread on my face. To quote a famous Dr. Suess book, "Oh, the thinks you can think."

"Ladies," I announced smugly, lifting up the closest incapacitated vampire by his collar. "Dinner's on me tonight."

Six

There were four of us and we could feed two per vampire. Though I wouldn't normally feed on a vampire, the blood of the Undead was very rich and we needed much less of it to be satisfied. Anyway, it seemed only fair that these two big-oted vamps who tried to kill us would end up being our meal. Imagine their embarrassment when they awoke to find our fang marks on their neck? Served them right.

I slipped on my headgear and heard Ileana snicker. I raised an eyebrow to her in question, but she said nothing. We all fed.

"We should drain them," Ileana spoke up after she drank her fill.

"Are you crathy?" I lisped.

"She's right," Angie agreed, surprising everyone. "They

will only try to kill us again. They shouldn't be allowed the chance."

They all looked toward me, the Protector in bright pink headgear, for guidance. Hey, I didn't want to get attacked again either, especially by vamps who might be more successful with their second attempt, but still, I didn't think it was right to drain them in cold blood.

I popped out my fangs and shook my head. "No, we leave them alive. There are laws governing behavior between vampires and none of us have acquired a blood-war license with these two. If they don't have ID, I'll take their picture with my cell phone and file charges with Carl when we get back to the house. Unless any of you want to carry them back?"

There was some grumbling, but all in all it was the right decision. Our existence was precarious at best. I hardly wanted to start a blood war with a vampire clan I knew nothing about. These two could have acted alone, or be part of a larger group. Either way, we survived the encounter relatively unharmed and victorious. That would send the right message. Half-bloods were not easy targets.

We hurried home and I told Carl everything that happened. The girls went downstairs to share the tale with Sage and Tina. It was very exciting, now that we were out of harm's way and I noticed they were exaggerating my combat prowess with each telling.

Carl took me aside to view the photos. I e-mailed them to him from the phone as well, but he didn't recognize them.

"So, it's started already," he murmured softly, careful to keep his tone hushed.

"You sound surprised."

"I am," he admitted, then clarified his position. "I'm not surprised someone would attack you—"

I snorted out a thanks but he continued, "I'm surprised it happened so soon. No one knows the House is occupied yet, Colby. The Tribunal's official position has always been that Psi Phi won't be inhabited by half-bloods for another two weeks."

"So what are you telling me?"

"I think we have a leak somewhere in the system," he said somberly.

"A leak? You mean a spy?" I whispered fiercely, looking around.

He nodded. "Either someone in our department is leaking information or one of the girls is not who she appears to be."

"Do you really think it could be one of them?" I was incredulous to say the least. I mean, did Carl ever bother to speak to any of the girls? They didn't seem the type.

"No, it's got to be someone in the department, Carl. I can't believe it's someone in the House."

"Are you saying that because you can't believe one of your own would turn against you?" he enjoyed mocking my naïveté.

"No, I mean none of them are smart enough to be a spy. Think about it, Carl. Tina wants to be a vegan vampire, for goodness' sake. Each candidate is as unlikely as the next."

Carl found himself nodding in agreement. It did seem unlikely. "We have to contact Thomas immediately," he said.

I knew he was right, of course. Thomas was senior in charge
and needed to know about this threat. However, I was the one
who'd averted disaster and saved the half-bloods. Surely that
counted for something?

"Fine, go ahead and call him. I'll go downstairs and hang
with my *sisters*. Maybe I'll learn a little more about their circumstances and get a better idea who's who down there."

I turned to leave but Carl stopped me by placing a hand
on my shoulder.

"Colby, you did well tonight."

I was shocked by his praise. Did Carl just compliment my
Protector skills? I nodded, afraid I would cry if I tried to ver-
bally respond. If only Thomas could see me the way Carl did,
as a competent Protector instead of a weak half-blood sidekick. I straightened my shoulders and shook it off. This was
no time to bemoan my relationship with Thomas. I had a spy
to catch.

Being a half-blood, I had many abilities that the average
vampire didn't have, such as being able to go out in the sunshine, as long as I didn't overdo the sun exposure and wore a
very high SPF. I discovered that several of my new housemates
did not possess this mutated ability. For instance, Angie and
Lucy were anti-sun. Ileana seemed happy to remain inside
and awake during the day but didn't mention if it was personal preference or basic survival.

I had incredible strength, but only at night. None of the

other girls claimed such ability. For the most part, I seemed to have more vampire attributes than my sorority sisters. They couldn't hear any better than a regular person and certainly couldn't distinguish odors the way I could.

"What about eye color, did any of you change eye color when it happened?" We were all hanging out in the basement, talking about the day we became Undead.

"My eyes have always been green, but I think they might be a deeper green now. I can't be sure. It's hard to remember," Ileana confessed.

"Hard to remember?" Angie questioned. "It's not like it happened a hundred years ago." And the group laughed.

Ileana smiled tightly in response, becoming silent once more when everyone else seemed to let information flow freely.

"Well, as you all know, my eyes are yellow now. They used to be gray. I have colored contacts my mom helped me pick out so I can go out without drawing too much attention."

"Your mom helped you pick them out?" Lucy asked, incredulously.

"Sure, she's pretty cool with the whole Undead thing."

The group was astounded that not only was I still in contact with my family, but they knew all about my vampire traits.

"My mama thinks I'm *el diablo*, the devil," Angie admitted softly, wiping a tear from her eye. "She told me to leave and never return, like I did something wrong, but it wasn't my fault." Her voice cracked but she pulled her composure together and said more forcefully, "It wasn't my fault."

"Of course it wasn't," Sage rushed to assure her. "We didn't ask to be different, to be Undead."

Tina piped up and stated, "I did." Effectively shocking the group.

"You did?" Lucy gasped.

"Yeah, I was hanging out at Cookie's a lot and I met this guy who surfed at night, which was way cool. Anyway, we started dating and I found out he was a vampire and I remember wishing in my head, ya know, that I could be like that. When I woke up, I was different, like a vampire but not."

I caught Sage's attention. She looked away quickly and I knew there was more to that story than Tina was revealing or even knew herself.

"What about you, Lucy?" I changed the subject and directed my question to the meekest one of the group. "What happened to you?"

"Oh, I guess it was my fault, really. I was walking home from work. I was trying to earn more money for college by working two jobs, you know." We nodded in agreement. Who didn't want more money? "Anyway, I worked at Starbucks during the day and took evening shifts at Dairy Queen. So I was walking home after the night shift, because I didn't have a car and we lived really close to the DQ. Anyway, this guy asked if I wanted a ride home and since he came into Starbucks all the time, I thought he would be safe, you know? I thought I *knew* him. But I guess I really didn't. Know him, that is."

We all stared at her, caught up in the story she was telling. It could have been any of us. Lucy wasn't frivolous or stupid. If anything, she was the most cautious of us all. She thought she knew this guy because she saw him at work all the time and he seemed so nice. It sounded like something I might do.

"What about you, Colby?" Ileana asked.

"How does one become the Protector of half-blood vampires and start a revolution?" Lucy added.

I was surprised she knew I'd started a revolution. It didn't seem like something the vampire guards would tell her while she rotted in a cell, but then, she could have easily picked up bits and pieces of the story around the House.

The girls all moved forward, eager to hear my tale. This was it. The moment I'd been waiting for since they first arrived. My moment to shine and finally accept the accolades I so richly deserved but when I started my story I realized it wasn't so unusual or unique. It was much like their stories, it just happened to me first. So I told them a revised-on-the-fly version instead.

"Well, actually the story of becoming Undead is not very exciting. I was stupid and walked home alone after a school game and was attacked by a rogue vampire. The real story lies with the victim before me, Jill Schneider. Now Jill was attacked a week before me and after that was visited by two very hot Vampire Investigators."

The group giggled and Angie blurted out "Carl, right?"

I nodded in her direction and Ileana added, in a singsong voice, "Thom-as." Which caused another round of laughter.

I winked at the group and continued, "So, Jill was taken in front of the Vampire Tribunal for the crime of being Undead without a license and she convinced two of the three leaders that she should exist and have a license."

"No," blurted Lucy, then she clapped a hand over her mouth.

I nodded in her direction. "She absolutely did."

Angie looked confused. "Why did she need a license? What was her crime?"

Tina interjected, "It wasn't her fault she was Undead, was it? She didn't ask to be a vampire, right?"

"Hmm, how to say this?" I thought aloud. "Once upon a time . . ." The group groaned but I silenced them with a look. "Vampires were a savage and primal species. The older the vampire, the more paranoid and crazy they became. They couldn't trust anyone because they thought everybody was out to get them. Eventually, blood wars between clans started to kill off the population and vampires wouldn't create more vampires because they were worried anyone they created would kill them. They were dying at an enormous rate.

"So, a few ancient vampires who still had most of their marbles decided the only way to save their kind was to create a more civilized ruling body—"

"The Tribunal!" Tina interjected and I nodded in agreement.

"Called the Tribunal. The three most powerful vampires would rule together. They required licenses to create new vampires and blood wars. You couldn't just go killing your vampire neighbor 'cause you felt like it. Investigators were hired to enforce the laws. Slowly, vampire populations started to stabilize. Other countries took notice and established their own Tribunals. The regulation of vampire creation is crucial because any vampire too many generations removed from the original bloodlines can not become sires. If they did, the half-bloods that were created were instantly killed. The Tribunal wanted only pure vampires to keep the race strong."

"So this girl convinced two of the most powerful vampires on the Tribunal to give half-bloods a chance?" Sage asked in awe.

I nodded.

"Then why are you the Protector and not her? What makes you so special?" Lucy questioned curiously.

"Jill was killed by our sire because she wanted to take her chance with the Tribunal and not join him to start his own clan. I simply picked up where she left off. I killed our Creator and convinced the third member of the Tribunal that half-bloods deserved a chance. That we were strong."

There was more to it of course, but I was hardly about to reveal the inner workings of my deal with the Tribunal and the role of Mr. Holloway in emancipating half-bloods. They knew as much as they needed to know.

"So you earned a license?" Angie asked.

"I did indeed." I put my right hand out for inspection, appreciating the "oohs" and "ahhs" from my fellow sisters.

"Can I try it on?" Tina asked eagerly.

Before I could reply Ileana answered in shock, "Of course not! A vampire never removes their license, ever. Only when they are dead does it come off."

The group gasped a collected "Ohhh!" and took a closer look at my ring but I wasn't paying any attention to them. I was staring at Ileana. Our eyes met for an instant, then she broke contact and pretended to make a great show of looking at my ring. How did she know that? Only a vampire would know that—wouldn't they?

After our gab session I was no closer to discovering a spy in the house than I was before, with the exception of Ileana, who seemed to know more about vampire politics than any of the others. But did that make her a spy? Who knew what kind of information she had access to in England. Maybe she had full reign of the vampire libraries back there.

I wandered upstairs after some of the girls decided to go to bed. Whereas I was used to sleeping a few hours at a time, everyone else seemed to prefer a good uninterrupted eight hours (or more).

I checked my e-mail and surfed the Internet for information about Ileana Romanav. She was mentioned on several royal genealogy sites. I reviewed her noble bloodlines and read brief excerpts pertaining to each generation but didn't come up with anything solid.

All I could find out of the ordinary was for the last four generations, the Romanav women married, had a daughter and then lost their mate shortly thereafter in some grisly catastrophe. One lost his head in a carriage accident, another was shot while hunting and a third died from a staph infection originating from a bug bite. Nothing by way of staking or puncture wounds to the neck.

I decided that since Piper was in England, she could do some checking for me. The Romanavs had several family estates and a few were open to the public for tours. I copied and pasted the ones I wanted Piper to go to and sent them in an e-mail. Hopefully she would have time to visit at least one or two and get any information that might be relevant. If Ileana was a spy, maybe Piper could uncover any local vampire lore surrounding the family.

After I sent the e-mail to Piper, I read and answered mail from Marci and Rachel. They were both going to college out of state and though we weren't nearly as close as we used to be, we still kept in touch. They thought I was tremendously cool to be starting a new sorority at PSU and both decided to rush this year at their prospective colleges. I wondered if other houses had similar setups as Psi Phi House but giggled at the thought. I doubted the feeding of its members would be as complicated as ours.

The bed seemed to beckon me and I changed into shorts and a tank top covered with cartoon fish that said "Sushi" and climbed into bed. I was very tired and knew Thomas would be home any time. I really didn't want to think about how that was going to go over. Sure we were fighting as a couple but it was the work thing that would make him the most upset.

I imagined the confrontation with Cookie was anything but pleasant. Suddenly I had a horrible thought. What if Cookie turned her vampire goons on him and he was attacked? Or worse, dead? I left him alone to face her and he could be chained in the basement at this very moment.

I jumped out of bed and raced downstairs to talk to Carl. I had to make sure Thomas was all right. I was in such a hurry, I practically stepped on Ileana's maid, sleeping on the floor outside Ileana's room.

"What the heck?" I muttered, awakening Sophie with my clumsiness.

"Mum?" she asked sleepily.

"What are you doing sleeping in the hallway?" I demanded, totally confused why she would do such a thing.

"I have always slept at my lady's door. It's my duty." She seemed to be a little more coherent.

"It's your duty? I thought it was your duty to take care of her. How can you do that if you don't get a good night's sleep?" I reasoned.

I wasn't going to take the "you deserve more" stance like before. This chick was way too brainwashed to think of herself as a separate entity.

"I can hear her better if I am close at hand," she stubbornly insisted.

"Whatever," I muttered, stepping past her to the stairs. I would worry about that wigged-out relationship later. Right now I had to make sure Thomas was okay.

Carl was nowhere in sight, which shouldn't have surprised

me because it was almost dawn. It was hard to remember other vampires couldn't be out in the sun, when I could.

I debated calling Thomas on the phone and decided against it. I didn't want to have our first conversation after such a big fight over a phone line. My puppy dog eyes and practiced pouty face would be far more effective in person.

I opted to call Carl instead.

"Carl here," he answered tersely.

"Hey Carl, it's me. Did you speak to Thomas yet?" I asked, pacing the living room.

"Why? Is something wrong?" Carl quickly jumped to the wrong conclusion.

"No, no. Everything's fine. I just . . . just wanted to know if you spoke to Thomas yet. Is he . . ." I paused and felt like an idiot checking up on him. He was a Tribunal Investigator, for crying out loud. A big boy who could take care of himself. "Is he aware of our situation?"

Boy, that didn't sound lame at all. Duh.

"Is he aware of our situation? Colby, are you sure you're all right?" Now Carl sounded very concerned.

I sighed heavily. Why was I so worried? Thomas could take care of himself way better than I could. Now I sounded like a mom obsessing over her little boy. Yuck, that was a really bad analogy and it totally creeped me out. I did not have motherly feelings toward Thomas at all. Blech.

"I just wanted to make sure he was safe, is all," I finally admitted.

Carl paused a moment and replied, "He is safe and will be home tonight."

"Good." I couldn't help feeling relieved.

"And Colby?"

"Yeah?"

"He needed to know you were safe as well."

I suppose that was supposed to make me feel all gooey inside but it had the exact opposite reaction. It was okay for me to worry at Thomas because I stranded him in California with no backup. It was not okay for Thomas to call Carl and check that I was safe back home at Psi Phi House. I mean, I managed to free two half-bloods without his help and he still felt the need to call and check up on me *in my own House*. As though I couldn't muddle through a couple days without him by my side, overseeing my every move?

I was upset with Thomas all over again. Yeah, I saw Piper's point and Carl made a good argument as well, but couldn't anyone see my side of the story, just this once? I looked out the window and thought I could catch the last remnants of sunrise if I hurried outside. Then maybe I could walk around and try to cool off.

I unlocked the door and stepped onto the porch. I ducked just in time to dodge the fist that came flying my way.

Seven

Without thinking, I reacted by driving my fist into my attacker's groin. He dropped like a ton of bricks.

"Sorry, sorry," he moaned over and over, hands clutching his crotch as he rolled side to side in pain.

It was a Tribunal Security guard. I turned at the sound of footsteps and found two more security guards racing up the porch with batons in hand.

They heard their partner wheezing, "My fault, sorry, oh God it hurts," and figured out the situation.

"What are you guys doing here?" I demanded.

"We were told to keep the perimeter secure by Investigator Thomas," replied one of the guards coming to the aid of his man on the floor.

"When did that come about?"

"We started detail this evening."

Thomas went so far as to assign a security detail to the house? He trusted my Protector skills so little he brought in a Tribunal Security team to do what he thought I was incapable of doing on my own?

They told me they were assigned as security during the day and hadn't expected any trouble; it was the night shift they believed would have all the action. The guy rolling on the floor was new and a bit nervous because the other two had told him all sorts of scary stories about the ferociousness of half-bloods. He was simply jumpy and when I opened the door without announcing my presence, he acted first and thought second. This, unfortunately for him, would be a decision that would haunt him for the rest of the day.

His two buddies helped pick him up and I rushed inside for a bag of ice. I didn't mean to punch so hard, but it was daytime so I hadn't thought I would do too much damage. I guess all those hours of training with Cyrus were improving my strength and reaction time.

I returned with the ice wrapped in a dish towel and apologized again.

"I'm really sorry about that," I clucked like a mother hen.

"Yeah, my bad. Not a problem," he responded through clenched teeth, yelping a little when he put the ice on his groin.

"I'm Colby, by the way." I put out my hand to shake but realized his were kind of full at the moment.

His two buddies grinned and introduced themselves as Todd and Mark, taking my hand in turn.

Todd, who'd explained the situation, was very tall and wide like a football linebacker. He whistled in appreciation of my fast reaction.

"You know, Colby, I've never seen a girl, much less such a tiny one such as yourself ever get the best of any Tribunal Security."

Mark nodded in agreement, looking at Zach, his downed comrade, in shame. "Yeah, it's a sad day when a girl punches you in the nads, man."

Zach tried to defend himself. "She's superfast and stronger than she looks."

I nodded at them. "He's right. I'm stronger than I look."

Todd and Mark looked at each other and laughed some more.

"It's okay, buddy." Todd clapped his hand on Zach's shoulder. "It can happen to the best of us."

There was more guffawing all around.

"If you guys hadn't told him all those stories about how dangerous half-bloods were, he wouldn't be hurt, you know."

I was trying to scold them but one look at Zach's face made me realize my mistake. The girl who punches a man's family jewels doesn't raise his standing by scolding his buddies. Apparently, this adds to the humiliation. So I decided to offer an olive branch instead.

"Zach?" I asked calmly. "Would it make things better between us if I knocked down your two friends and then you guys would all be on an even footing?"

Zach replied tightly, "It sure would be a nice start." And

his two buddies starting laughing even harder, which worked out great for me because they didn't even see it coming.

I was already in a crouched position, so I launched myself straight up at the two on the stairs and struck both of their windpipes at the same time. They lost their breath, leaned forward and grabbed their throats in a vain attempt to protect against another strike and then I took both of their heads and smacked them together. I tempered my strength so I wouldn't knock them out or cause any serious pain, but enough that they felt it and Zach could be redeemed.

"Better?" I asked Zach.

"Much," he replied smugly.

I turned back to the door and entered the house. "Good night gentlemen," I tossed over my shoulder and was rewarded by the sound of a downed guard vomiting on the porch.

Shaking my head in exasperation, I headed back upstairs. I was still mad at Thomas but after meeting my protection, I was not convinced Curly, Larry and Moe were going to be much help. Still, they would make some noise if attacked and that was something.

I stepped over Sophie's sleeping form and crawled back into bed. I felt better after sparring with the guards but was still upset at Thomas.

*   *   *

When I awoke again, it was early evening. I brushed my teeth and showered. Nothing felt as good as a warm shower when you're Undead. The hot spray warmed my cool body up and

I almost felt alive. I stepped out of the shower and was surprised to see Angie getting ready to jump in a shower stall as well.

"Did you sleep well?" I asked her.

"Like the dead," she quipped and I laughed. You gotta like a girl who doesn't take herself too seriously.

I changed into stretch denim capri pants—low-rise, naturally—and a pink half-shirt that said "Barely Legal."

My dad hated that shirt. Piper got it for me on my birthday. I did the makeup thing—a hint of blush, a swish of lip gloss—and popped in my colored contacts. I pulled my hair up in two braids, one over each ear, and gave myself the once-over in the mirror. I could so pull off the naughty schoolgirl look. Satisfied, I made my way downstairs.

I looked around for someone who could go outside, but I couldn't find Tina and Sage was still sleeping. I decided to feed early, before the sun went down. I walked to the door and announced that I was coming outside, giggling to myself.

When I opened the door and peeked out, Zach was nowhere to be seen but Todd was on the porch.

"Can I come out?" I asked.

He snorted at me. "Like I could stop you?"

"Oh, come on, don't be sore. I had to do it. You guys would never let poor Zach live it down if I hadn't."

I gave him my best pouty girl look and he caved. That's right; they always cave for the pouty girl.

"I'm going to take a walk," I told him, stepping onto the porch.

He shook his head at me. "Sorry, Colby, no can do. No one can leave the premises without an escort."

"Even during the day?" I asked in surprise.

"Affirmative. Thomas's orders," he replied.

"Okay, can you be my escort?"

He looked a bit uncertain, so I reassured him. "I don't bite," I teased, then slapped my hand over my mouth in chagrin. I couldn't believe I just said that.

He laughed at me and reported into his walkie-talkie that he was escorting me around the block and would check back in twenty minutes.

We left together and I steered him toward the park.

"So," he said, "where did you learn . . ."

His voice trailed off and I piped up tartly, "How to kick your ass so effectively?"

He gave me a pained expression and nodded.

"I'm the Protector. It's my job. How 'bout you? Gotta admit, you have a pretty odd job. What with being human and all."

He looked at me in surprise. "You're not human anymore?"

I smiled ruefully at him. "Not technically. I'm more vampire but not fully blooded."

We walked in compatible silence for awhile. I was enjoying the coolness in the air and the sun dropping down, casting a kaleidoscope of colors across the horizon. I inhaled the scent of berries, freshly cut lawns and soft ocean spray on the air.

Todd looked at me funny. I knew he could smell none of

the odors I was enjoying so I shrugged in his direction. It didn't matter anyway.

He surprised me by finally answering my question. "A friend told me about this job after I graduated college. I used to play football but wasn't good enough for the big time and security sounded kind of interesting. Especially this kind of stuff."

"Babysitting a bunch of girls in a sorority house is interesting, huh?" I teased him and he smiled.

"Well, not until this morning it wasn't. But I never knew about your kind before. I mean vampires. I had no idea they walked among us and all. It's been an eye-opening experience, I can tell you."

I nodded in agreement. It had been for me as well. But I was puzzled why the Tribunal employed human security guards and posed the question to him.

"You guys can only operate during the night. We can do things during the day, like transport and investigating."

"And do it under the cover of daylight, without being thwarted by other vampires?" I was starting to understand. Pretty smart, actually.

"I used to do mostly transport of mutant, er, half-bloods," he corrected himself quickly, "but I guess that will all change soon. I hope I don't lose my job." He frowned at the thought.

I tucked my arm through his and squeezed gently. "I don't think you have to worry about job security. We aren't going anywhere and we're certainly not the most popular girls in the Undead community."

I was the queen of understatement.

He patted my hand and kept it through his arm and we walked in compatible silence. Todd was a nice guy and he was there to protect me. But he also knew I could protect myself. He respected that ability in me, unlike Thomas. It was kind of nice; I hadn't been able to walk arm in arm and admire the sunset in a long time. He was no Thomas, but I wasn't all that thrilled with Thomas right now.

I sighed heavily and Todd looked at me in question. "It's nothing. Life is complicated," I said.

He smiled teasingly. "Boyfriend?"

"At this point, I'm not sure." And the thing of it was, I *wasn't* sure. If we didn't have mutual respect of our abilities, what did we have? We didn't have the physical side. I sighed again.

We rounded the block and a Starbucks came into view. It was teeming with coeds desperately needing caffeine.

"Why don't you go get a latte, I'll be right around here."

He shook his head, "I can't do that, Colby. I have strict orders you're not to leave my sight."

"You know what I need to do though, don't you?"

He shifted uneasily. "I think I get the gist of it. It's no big deal, Colby. You have to do what you have to do."

"I won't do that in front of you, Todd. But you're right, I *have* to do it."

"How about a compromise? You find, er, someone and I'll be your lookout. I promise I won't peek. I'll just be close at hand if you need me."

I nibbled on my lower lip in indecision. I hated feeding in

general and I certainly didn't want Todd the Rent-a-Cop watching me do it—but what choice did I have?

"Okay fine. Do you want a coffee?"

He nodded in agreement and we went inside the store. It was cool and calming. I loved the way Starbucks decorated their stores. And the aroma of flavors. Intoxicating. I could smell a Starbucks a block away.

There was a pleasant-enough guy behind us in line. He had a newspaper and wore cutoffs. While Todd was ordering his drink, I spoke to the gentleman and he nodded, as though in a trance.

Todd waited for his coffee and I enjoyed the hustle and bustle of people. When his order was ready, I directed him outside and to the side of the store. There were large Dumpsters next to the building and it was slightly exposed but if Todd was acting as my lookout, I didn't need anything more secluded.

Todd asked me what we were doing; I told him we were waiting for someone. Sure enough, my new friend left the coffeehouse, cappuccino in hand, and joined us. I beckoned him further into the shadows. After Todd was satisfied I was in no danger, he turned his back to me.

I studied my victim for a moment and then slipped my headgear into place. His eyes widened a moment but he didn't move. I gently tilted his head to one side and whispered, "Everything is going to be okay," then sank my fangs into his neck.

I closed my eyes and drank, holding him upright and steady, close to me. I discovered early on that some people fainted when I was feeding, not because they were in pain or I was drinking too much, just that their blood pressure dropped suddenly. Now I held them close, to avoid hurting them.

When I was done, I licked across the wound and it instantly healed. I pulled off my fangs and looked deep into his eyes. I told him to forget our meeting and have a great day. He wandered away slowly, still in a bit of a daze. Once he entered the busy courtyard he seemed to shake out of the trance I'd put him under and went about his business.

I looked at Todd and found him staring at me in open-mouthed disbelief.

"You watched me!" I accused, angry he'd broken his promise.

He took several strides in my direction. "I had to make sure you were safe, Colby."

"You lied to me," I hissed at him, trying to pass him by.

He grabbed me by the arms and said, "Don't make a scene. I'm sorry I lied to you, really I am, but your safety is my number-one concern."

"It changes everything now, don't you see?" I was fighting with tears. Todd was a nice guy and we were getting along so well. I was hoping he would want to be my friend, but now that was impossible.

"Why does it change everything? I don't understand. Help me understand, Colby."

"I thought we could be friends. But now you've see me as some dark creature who feasts on human blood and that changes *everything*."

I wanted to storm away but part of me hoped he would understand. That he wouldn't think I was so terrible.

"I don't think you're some freak at all. You're just different. You didn't hurt that guy, you were very nice. Almost reverent in how you treated him. He'll never know he played a part in your life and that makes me a little sad, for him."

"Huh?" I was so not prepared for this speech.

"Here we are. Two species existing together but one of us has no idea the other exists. Like we're on two separate plains. Your kind depends on us, needs us to survive, but we'll never know your culture, who you really are or your sense of humor." He touched my cheek and I smiled in spite of myself.

"It seems like a small price to pay for getting to know you better. Really understanding you." His mouth was moving closer to mine and I was caught up in what he was saying. I didn't disgust him. He wanted to know my kind better. He wanted to know *me* better. He respected my Protector skills. Even though he knew what I was, he wasn't afraid of me or disgusted by me. When his lips drew close to mine, I didn't resist. After all, Thomas didn't want me. I leaned into the kiss.

Eight

His lips touched mine. I realized too late I'd just fed and my mouth was still warm with blood. Todd didn't seem to mind; in fact he deepened the kiss immediately. He wrapped his arms around me and I let him hold me. He tasted like caramel and coffee and for a moment I didn't think about Thomas or my responsibilities as Protector. I just lived in the moment. Todd ended the kiss and held me, softly kissing my jawline, and whispered in my ear, "Bite me, Colby. Let me give you what you need."

I jumped away as though burned. What kind of sicko game was this? Todd didn't have the hots for me! He had the hots for *vampires*. Ewwwwww.

"Leave me alone," I commanded and he nodded, entranced by my command.

I ran away from him toward the park, wiping my mouth with the back of my hand. *I can't believe I kissed him and let him hold me!* He probably got his jollies while watching me feed on the other guy.

I hated this! I hated being different and living in a human world where people didn't understand or they got excited at the thought of feeding us. For the first time since I became Undead I doubted I could do it. Stay Undead, that is. It would either break my spirit or drive me crazy and that scared me more than any vampire with a grudge ever could. Thomas was the only one who understood and I could hardly share my confusion over this experience. With Piper in Europe, I'd never felt more alone.

It was well after dark when I finally made my way back to Psi Phi House. I still didn't know what I was going to do. What could I do? I had to find a way to cope with all these feelings, but who could I turn to? My parents wouldn't understand, vampires certainly wouldn't understand. Maybe there was a reason half-bloods weren't allowed to exist before now. Maybe someone, somewhere in time figured out how hard it would be for us and made the merciful decision to snuff us out of existence.

No! My mind railed against that treacherous thought. We did deserve to exist, we could survive. I was not giving up hope yet. I rounded the corner, just as two cars pulled up to the House. I recognized Mr. Holloway and Thomas immediately, but the occupants of the other car were strangers to me.

I slowed down and greeted Mr. Holloway politely, nodded

to Thomas and waited to be introduced to the others. I hadn't met them yet but I had a pretty good idea the lady in question was Cookie Flannegan and one of the gentlemen with her, sporting streaked blond hair and a Hawaiian shirt, was probably Lance, Tina's ex-boyfriend.

Boy, my day was just getting better and better.

"Is this her?" Cookie demanded, ignoring, yet again, my hand to shake. I really was beginning to think I was lord of the Undead lepers.

"This is Colby Blanchard, the half-blood Protector," Mr. Holloway confirmed, giving me credence by introducing me using my full title. I really wished I'd rethought the braids and "Barely Legal" shirt.

"Where are they?!" she demanded, shaking her finger at me.

"I assume you mean Tina and Sage? They're inside," I responded politely, resisting the urge to grab her finger. Why did every vampire I met have such bad manners?

"Charles, I want them home. I want them on the next flight back to California with me," Cookie demanded, and I widened my eyes in surprise. No one I knew talked to Mr. Holloway in such a familiar manner. That is, no one but me.

I was waiting for the deep freeze when he surprised me with a gentle rebuff. "Now, Cookie, you know the law. The girls are staying at Psi Phi House. I know it's difficult for you but that is the way things are going to be."

Cookie seemed to crumble a bit under his stern kindness and I noted the tears glistening in her blue eyes. "But I didn't even get to say good-bye," she whispered brokenly.

Uh, these were not the actions of a wicked vampire slave master. These were the actions of a mother who'd had her children taken from her. Uh-oh. What was the deal here? What had I done?

"Let's all step inside, if you please," I suggested, taking the despondent Cookie by the elbow and guiding her onto the porch.

I glanced at Thomas, whose expression was devoid of emotion, except for the clenched jaw and muscle ticking by his ear. We entered the house and I immediately went in search of Tina and Sage. I found Sage upstairs and told her Cookie was here to see her and she squealed with delight. She pushed past me to greet her and I had the sinking feeling this was going to turn out very badly . . . for me.

I saw Sophie and asked if she'd seen Tina.

"Not since yesterday, mum."

I made the rounds upstairs, knocking on doors and getting no response. I hurried downstairs to witness Sage and Cookie hugging each other and Sage telling her all about her adventures to date. Including the attack by vampires, which had Cookie checking her over from head to toe to make sure she was truly safe. The look she shot me was pure venom. How dare I put her little girl in danger, it seemed to say.

I smiled weakly and hurried to the library. I slipped inside the bookcase and called to Tina. Where was she?

I found Angie watching reruns of *Buffy* and asked if she'd seen Tina.

"Nope, not since yesterday. She was on the computer after

Lucy when I went to bed. Colby, isn't this hysterical? Look at their faces! They have no idea what a vampire really looks like. Too funny."

I ignored her and stepped into the sleeping dorm. I noted two beds were unmade, and assumed they were Lucy and Angie's. I opened the door to the next partition and found one bed slightly askew, but the others were perfectly made up. Had Tina slept down here last night or had she gone upstairs?

I hurried out of the dorm and asked Angie, "Where did you sleep last night?"

"In the first bed. I didn't make it yet. Is that okay?" She seemed concerned, especially after seeing the expression on my face.

"I can't seem to find Tina," I told her and she immediately jumped up to help me look.

"She probably slept upstairs and didn't hear you call her," Angie tried to reassure me but I was beginning to panic. Something wasn't right, I could feel it.

We made our way to the main living room, where Cookie demanded to know where Tina was.

"Still looking, ma'am. I'm going back upstairs to check again."

"What's going on?" Lucy asked, cup of tea in hand as she wandered in from the kitchen.

"We're looking for Tina, have you seen her?" Angie asked. Lucy shook her head no.

I took the steps two at a time and this time I opened each room to look, I didn't just call her name.

The first bedroom was filled with excess furniture that Ileana had moved from her room, but no Tina. The next room was empty. Ileana's room was also empty, unless you counted Ileana and Sophie, both a little miffed that I just barged in. Neither had seen Tina.

Next to her was Lucy and Angie's room; no luck there so I took a deep breath and pushed open Sage and Tina's bedroom door. To my surprise it was empty as well. Where could she be?

I quickly searched the bathroom and showers, then my room. Where could she be?

"Did she go to feed or something?" I asked the girls. I turned to Thomas, who'd followed behind me. "Check with Security and see if she left with one of them." Thomas immediately snapped open his cell phone and walked down the hall to check it out.

I looked at the concerned faces of the girls in front of me and felt a cold dread slip up my spine. There was one room I hadn't checked. Slowly, almost like I was hypnotized, I walked past each of them and down the stairs. The look on my face must have been something because Cookie was in mid-complaint and stopped when she saw me. I turned away from her and walked back toward the only bedroom I hadn't checked, the housemother's room. I opened the door slowly and clicked on the light. Everything was quiet and looked undisturbed but I knew, I knew in my heart that she was here.

I stepped over to Ileana's trunks and pulled the smaller one off the top. I carelessly flung it over my shoulder; it bounced on the bed, then hit the floor.

Ileana had just joined the group and scolded, "Hey, those are my things you're throwing about. Have a care, will you?" But I ignored her. I took the next two trunks and flung them aside with equal disregard. They were empty and easily tossed. The bottom trunk was quite large. Large enough for a wardrobe full of clothes or for a body. I grasped the handle on one side and lifted. It was heavy and I gently laid it back down.

I shook as I popped open the latch. *Please no, please no, please no,* I chanted in my head. *Let me be wrong about this, please,* I begged to myself.

I lifted the trunk lid and laid out before me, her legs folded up as though she were sitting in a chair, was Tina. She wore a halter top, flowing skirt and socks. She looked unharmed except for the puncture marks at her throat. She'd been drained of all her blood. She was dead.

The scream that erupted from Cookie's throat reverberated in my head long after she broke down in sobbing hysterics. No parent should have to see their child like this. I leaned forward, turning Tina's head gently to get a better view of the puncture wounds.

Cookie erupted again. "Get your hands off her! Don't you touch her! You killed her, you hear me! I hold you responsible. You killed her!" She broke down again as Mr. Holloway and Carl pulled her gently from the room. She collapsed in hysteria, clutching Sage like a doll to her chest. They cried together, comforting each other as best they could.

Thomas ushered the rest of the girls out of the room and closed the door, leaving us alone with Tina.

"I don't understand how she died," I wondered aloud. "I thought the only way to kill a vampire was to stake them in the heart or decapitate them. Our blood doesn't move that fast, how could she be drained?"

Thomas kneeled down next to me and examined her ankles. Beneath the socks—and really I should have picked up on that right away as Tina never wore socks—her ankles were red and angry.

"Rope burns," I whispered.

Thomas nodded grimly.

I sank down on the corner of the bed and pushed the hair that escaped from its braids off of my sweaty brow. I was feeling very woozy. Thomas recapped what we knew.

"Okay, sometime after Angie saw her on the computer, someone fed off of her, tied her feet and hoisted her overhead to drain her. But they didn't do it here." He motioned toward the ceiling. "There isn't a pulley that could be rigged in this room. They must have moved her to this room after they were through."

"The showers," I whispered. "They did it in one of the shower stalls and after that, dressed her back up and brought her downstairs to this room, putting her in the bottom trunk. Then they stacked the other trunks up so it didn't look disturbed."

"Why? Why go through all of that to kill a half-blood? Doesn't it serve a better purpose to leave her where the girls would find her? That sends a more powerful message."

"I don't think we were supposed to find her, Thomas. I think we were supposed to think she ran away, went back to California or wherever. Someone went to an awful lot of trouble to keep this hidden and tidy."

Thomas looked back at Tina and gently shut the trunk lid. I sat on the bed, staring at it. I whispered softly, "This was my fault. Cookie's right. I might as well have killed Tina myself. I brought her here, into danger. I failed to protect her. She's dead because of me."

Thomas sat down next to me and put his arm around me. "It's not your fault, Colby," he tried to comfort me, but it was no use. We both knew better.

"I'm not sure I can do this, Thomas," I said in a small, empty voice that didn't sound like me at all.

"Colby, you're in shock. Let me take you upstairs to your room to lie down." He tried to get me to stand but I couldn't. I was numb all over.

"I just can't. I'm not cut out for this. Don't you see I'm only a kid? All I wanted to do was go to college and live in a sorority like other girls. I never asked for any of this. You were right all along. I can't protect anyone." I felt helpless, like I was drowning.

Thomas dropped down in front of me and took my face in his hands. "Colby? Listen to me very carefully. We'll get through this. We will. I know you didn't ask for this but you're the strongest person I know. You're not like the other girls. You're special. Colby, you might not like it but I know you can do this."

I stared into his eyes and in their depths I could see he meant what he said. He believed in me. And it was that belief that helped me rally past the suffocating guilt and depression. I was the Protector. I didn't ask for the job, didn't even want the job, but it was mine all the same.

Nine

Thomas and I left the back room to join the others. The girls were subdued; Sage was still struggling with her grief. Cookie had pulled herself together and was rocking Sage back and forth on the couch, clucking and softly hushing Sage's tears. I never wanted my mother more than I did at that moment.

I needed her to hold me and tell me everything was going to be okay and take control of the situation so I wouldn't have to deal. But I knew better. This was my responsibility. Growing up had never hurt so much.

Mr. Holloway was out on the porch with the men who'd escorted Cookie here. Carl was standing by the door; I couldn't tell if he was there to keep us from leaving or keep anyone from entering. Either way, I was glad to see him.

Thomas looked at me as though in question and I nodded. I would address the group. They were my responsibility.

"As you all know, we found Tina in . . ." I cleared my throat. "We found Tina." It was not an auspicious start for me. "Thomas and I have ascertained the cause of death and need to ask each of you some questions. We believe someone managed to get into the House and commit this crime so we need everyone to cooperate with the questioning."

Thomas looked at me in speculation, but I kept searching the faces of each of the girls in the room. I didn't believe for a moment that someone broke into the House and killed Tina. I believed it was one of the girls before me, but I wanted her to think she was safe, above suspicion. I wanted her to get cocky and make a mistake that would lead us to her.

"Now, when was the last time each of you saw Tina?" I started with Sophie. She was human so I knew she couldn't have bitten Tina, but she *was* Ileana's loyal maid and would do anything Ileana asked her to do, including disposing of Tina.

"I saw her briefly after my lady came to bed. She walked down the hallway with Sage. They said they were headed downstairs to watch a spot of tellie."

"And that was the last time you saw her?"

"Yes, mum." Her head bobbed.

"Thank you, Sophie. Ileana, was that the same time you saw her?"

"Actually, I didn't see her at all. I was inside my room. I heard her talk to Sophie, though, through the door."

I nodded. "How about you, Angie?"

"I was watching television and Lucy was on the computer when Sage and Tina joined us. I went to bed about an hour later."

"Did you go upstairs first?"

She nodded. "Yes, I went upstairs to take my makeup off and brush my teeth. I wore my sweats and tank top to bed."

"Did you see Sophie when you went to bed?"

Angie wrinkled her forehead. "No, I don't think so. I was pretty dog tired, though."

Sophie looked guilty, stealing sideway glances toward Ileana, who completely ignored her and appeared bored by the entire questioning.

"Thanks, Angie. How about you, Lucy?"

"I went to bed right after Angie. I didn't go upstairs because I brushed my teeth earlier and was already in my pajamas."

"Angie, did you hear Lucy come to bed?"

She shook her head no. "But I'm a pretty heavy sleeper."

"Sage, when did you last see Tina?"

"I went upstairs to get a milkshake. Tina was on the computer. When I went back downstairs, she wasn't there. I assumed she went upstairs to go to bed, even though we're supposed to sleep in the dormitory." She bit her lip to keep it from trembling. "She wanted to sleep under the window so she could see the sky."

"Did you see or meet anyone while you were in the kitchen?"

Sage shot a quick look toward Sophie, who was practically rolled into a ball on the couch, trying to look invisible.

"I saw Sophie in the kitchen."

I was hardly surprised, Sophie reeked of guilt. I could smell her deceit a mile away.

"Oh mum, I'm so sorry I left my post. I really am. You were sound asleep and I was so thirsty. There isn't anything to drink around here and I saw Sage bring back groceries from the store. She had ice cream and milk and offered to make milkshakes for everyone," she practically wailed. "I only left for a short time. I promise."

Ileana looked at her disapprovingly, but said nothing. Sophie looked like she was going to have a heart attack over the indiscretion. I exchanged a look with Thomas. I think we could rule out Sophie being a coconspirator if a stolen milkshake caused this type of commotion.

"It's okay, Sophie. No one cares if you enjoyed a milkshake with Sage. Ileana's fine with it, aren't you, Ileana?"

She pursed her lips together disapprovingly and we locked eyes for a moment. Finally she relented and patted poor Sophie on the arm. "Of course I don't mind, Sophie. I'm not a monster, you know. I'm happy you took a break."

"Oh, thank you, mum," Sophie gushed and I couldn't help but curl my lip in distaste. This poor woman was worse than a lapdog that piddled on the carpet. *Just rub her nose in it and forgive her already. It's just a freakin' milkshake.*

"Thank you, everyone, you can leave. However, be advised that no one is to leave the House without a security escort for the time being."

They all were starting to get up when Cookie demanded,

"What about you? When was the last time you saw my Tina?"

I looked over at Thomas as everyone sort of froze in place. Me? Did she think I went all the way to California to bring Sage and Tina back just so I could off one of them here? But it got me thinking—when did I last see Tina, anyway? Was it before I went outside and had my run-in with Tribunal Security?

"Actually, the last time I saw her was when we were all talking downstairs. I went upstairs to check e-mail from my laptop and surf the Net. I tripped over Sophie around dawn but didn't see anyone else. I called Carl from my cell then went back to bed." I omitted the Security confrontation. If they knew Security was watching the house during the day, they would never buy my break-in story.

Cookie glared at me, but said no more. That seemed to be the sign for everyone to go about their business. Mr. Holloway gathered Carl, Thomas and me for a quick meeting. The only place we could go out of earshot was outside or in the bedroom where Tina rested. And I really didn't want to go back in there.

We went out the back door, which was heavily bolted, and stood on the concrete patio slab overlooking the alley behind the house. The backyard was basically extra parking, but none of us owned a car at the moment.

"Hell of a first week on the job, Colby," Mr. Holloway murmured.

Thomas and Carl were quick to jump to my defense but

I waved them aside. This was my responsibility and I wasn't going to let them take the brunt of Mr. Holloway's displeasure.

"It's certainly been a learning experience, sir."

He looked me over and clapped his hand on my shoulder. "You're holding up remarkably well, under the circumstances."

It was the closest thing to praise I was likely to get and I much preferred that to screaming about my incompetence.

"A determined vampire could probably find his way inside the house if he really wanted to," Mr. Holloway remarked and I snorted at him.

"One of the girls did it, sir. We both know that."

He nodded in agreement and asked, "Any guesses as to who's responsible?"

I debated how much to reveal and opted for the truth. "I am, sir. I didn't kill Tina, but it happened on my shift all the same. I'll find the killer."

He nodded sagely. "I have faith in you. Keep me abreast of your progress." He walked to the door and opened it, then paused to add, "And Colby, the shopping trip was the right move. Those two girls should not have been treated like that. Rest assured we are investigating the matter."

And then he left us standing outside under the night sky.

"Come on, Colby," Thomas said, pulling my hand and leading me through the backyard.

"Where are we going?" I asked, looking back at Carl, who followed Mr. Holloway into the house.

"To get a break from all this."

He led me to his car and opened the door. I was grateful to

be away from Psi Phi House for a respite but wasn't sure if being alone with Thomas was the best medicine right now. Things weren't right between us and I just couldn't take another emotional confrontation.

He slid into the driver's side and started the car. The '68 Mustang rumbled to life and Thomas eased onto the side street. It only took a few moments to reach the freeway and soon we were barreling south on Interstate 5.

"What about Tina's body?" I asked quietly.

"I've got Carl taking care of all that." And we both stopped talking.

The silence was pretty heavy in the car; Thomas didn't turn on the radio and neither did I. What kind of music do you listen to when you're investigating a murder? It hardly seemed appropriate to blast Coldplay and the thought of Avril's angst seemed shallow. I mean, did Avril ever have to investigate a vampire death? I think not.

I closed my eyes, ignoring the scenery whizzing by. I would just let Thomas handle it. It felt good to release control to someone who clearly loved to be in charge. Thomas pulled off the freeway at the south end of town, stopping the car in a large, deserted parking lot.

"Thomas?" I asked in question. This wasn't my first choice for a feeding ground. It was the parking lot to the Fun Park, which didn't appear to be much fun, judging by the lack of occupants.

"I am taking you miniature golfing," he announced, catching me by surprise.

"Miniature golfing? Why?"

"Because that's what normal couples do. They make plans to do activities together. Activities that don't include dodging swords, memorizing vampire law or investigating half-blood murders."

The man had a point there.

I gracefully submitted to his proposal and followed him to the front gate.

"Are they open?" I wondered aloud, not seeing any activity inside the building.

"The golf course is open to one A.M. tonight. I called ahead."

I nodded in agreement. Of course he did. That's what Thomas did. He made things happen by cell phone. It was one of the things I admired about him. That and his tight rear end, which I was enjoying an unobstructed view of at the moment. Thomas was old school in many ways, including his taste in clothes. Sure, he could do the layered shirt thing with the best of them but he believed that jeans should fit and fit well. No baggy pants for him and really, who could ask for more in a boyfriend?

After paying for nine holes, Thomas escorted me to the first green, a curvy sort of grass corridor leading into a windmill. The trick was to time your stroke so the ball missed the arms of the spinning fan. So easy a child could do it, right?

"You go first," I insisted and he positioned himself above the ball.

"Have you ever golfed before?" he asked, carefully lining up his aim.

"No, I can honestly say this is my first time," I admitted as he followed through and sent the little ball straight toward the windmill and directly into the tower. A hole in one.

"I'll try to be gentle," he teased softly, looking over his shoulder at me.

I smirked at him then turned my head away toward the entrance. Joking about first times made me remember our fight back in California. Piper had helped me see that I'd been pretty hurtful and childish. Immature, to coin a better term.

"You know, Thomas, I'm sorry about—"

He held up his hand to stop my apology. "No, we're not going there right now. Now we're embroiled in the greatest game ever played."

I giggled at his dramatization. "Greatest game ever played, huh? Miniature golf?"

He shrugged his shoulders and clarified, "Well, golf in any form is a pretty perfect sport."

I took my turn on the putting green and grunted. Thomas and my dad were a match made in heaven.

"Choke up a little on the club," he coached and when I didn't do it to his satisfaction he stepped forward to position my hands himself.

He held me from behind in a semiembrace, hands over mine, and led me through the motions of the stroke. I easily could have spent the entire night deliberately misunderstanding his pointers just to feel his body every time he corrected me. I loved the way he smelled like chocolate chip cookies, and the one thing I wanted more than anything was for things to be right between us and for him to kiss me.

"There you go. Not bad at all," he murmured in my hair after guiding me through the swing. My eyes were closed and I was leaning back into him, not paying any attention to the ball, but I agreed with him nonetheless, "Mmmmm, not bad at all."

He abruptly stepped away and I swayed a little, quickly righting myself. Was it fair to change a sixteen-year-old girl into a vampire, leaving her a perpetual hormonal mess for all of eternity? I think not. How could I concentrate on this stupid game if he was going to invade my personal space like that?

I lined up my second shot and hit it much harder than was appropriate, shooting the ball over two greens and past the sixth hole.

"Sorry," I muttered.

We trotted off to the next course. This one required skipping the ball over a couple of islands surrounded by a foot of water and landing the ball on a lily pad, which was guarded by a jumping frog. I marveled at the skill it would take to achieve a hole in one and thought, *Who came up with these stupid courses, anyway?*

"I'll let you go first this time," Thomas gallantly offered.

As I walked past him to the tee, I smartly retorted, "It seems you're a little fast and loose with the rules of the greatest game ever played, aren't you?"

"Maybe I just like the scenery from back here." He offered this confession in a hushed tone and I practically whacked the fake grass off the concrete.

"Are you doing that on purpose?" I accused, shaking out my arm, which was still vibrating from the club striking the ground.

"Who, me?" he declared, wide-eyed and innocent, taking his turn with the ball. I watched in silence as he gently struck and it bounced not once, but twice and landed perfectly on the next island. We were walking over the bridge that connected the small land when I blurted out, "Have you ever wanted to bite me?"

Thomas was just stepping down from the bridge when I asked, and he tripped over the edge, stumbling into the pond.

Ten

"Thomas, are you okay?" I rushed over to help him.

"What makes you ask a thing like that?" he demanded, struggling to escape the pond without getting his other foot wet. I grabbed his hand and pulled him toward me.

"Well, I just wondered if you ever felt like biting me. Like in the heat of the moment or anything." If my face could burn with shame, it would be a deep shade of crimson.

"Colby?" Thomas asked, using his exasperated-but-must-have-details voice.

"I've heard some people, some *living* people think that it's sort of a turn-on. Getting bit by a vampire." I peeked through my lashes to check out his face.

He definitely looked uncomfortable with the turn our conversation was taking.

"Who did you hear that from?"

I blew out my breath and confessed, "One of the Tribunal Security guards. Is it true, then?"

Thomas ran his fingers through his soft brown hair and then massaged the back of his neck, obviously trying to think of how to say what he was going to say in a way I would understand.

"Well?" I prompted, starting to enjoy his discomfort.

"Well, yes. Some living and Undead enjoy the art of biting when, uh, experiencing certain intimate acts and uh, maybe I have been known to think, uh, certain thoughts about you in, uh, that way." He finished talking and looked like he was going to faint.

"So, is that a yes then?" I questioned, looking for some clarification on the subject.

He looked at the ground, his wet pant leg and then the club. I was watching him pretty intently and thought I caught a quick affirmative nod.

"And that doesn't strike you as a little gross? Feeding on your girlfriend?" I was certainly puzzled by the appeal.

"Col-by." He was using that tone again and drawing out my name to sound more like a groan. Hey, I wasn't the one with perverted biting fantasies here.

"Can we talk about this someplace more private please?" he pleaded and I turned to look around.

"We're the only ones here, Thomas. It doesn't get much more private than total isolation." Really, the man had no sense of timing at all.

Finally, he gave up speaking to me altogether and pulled me roughly into his arms. *Yeah baby.* His mouth was on mine and I dropped the stupid club and threw my arms around his neck. We were pressed so closely together I could feel every outline of his body—and I mean every outline. The guy was happy to see me, if you know what I mean.

His tongue was dancing with mine, his hands were all over my back, my shoulders and my butt. After much heated making out, he smoothed his hands over my braids, captured my face and rained kisses over my lips, jawline and neck. I gripped his shoulders tightly, pulling him closer; but it was impossible to get any closer to him than I was.

I felt his mouth open and wanted to warn him not to give me a hickey (because really, they make you look so cheap) and gasped when I felt his fangs pierce my skin. This wasn't like before, when I was attacked and brutally bitten. This was sexy, erotic and a total turn-on.

My back arched and I moaned his name. It felt like every romance novel I ever read. Okay, so I've read a few steamy vampire books. Like you haven't?

This wasn't disgusting or painful or mere feeding. This was passion between two consenting Undead. And it was HOT!

"Thomas," I moaned again, causing him to pause and take stock of his surroundings. We were in the middle of a miniature golf island and I'd practically wrapped my legs around his waist trying to get closer to him. We might have privacy to talk but I believe we were still in full view of the freeway.

He licked my neck to seal the wound and I shivered in

delight. "Come on," he said, grabbing my hand and practically flinging me toward the gate, our clubs all but forgotten by the faux frog pond. It was a mad dash to the car, with Thomas fumbling for his keys to put in the lock.

He pulled the door open with such force, he hit his knee and swore under his breath. I giggled a little watching him try to put the key in the ignition. On his third attempt, he was successful and revved the engine to life. We broke every speeding law in our haste to find privacy, true privacy. He pulled off the freeway and within two blocks, we were parked in a small numbered lot next to a quaint brownstone in the Beacon Hill area.

I was suitably cooled down by now and realized this was the first time I'd ever been to Thomas's apartment. He led me to the security entrance and we walked to the end of the corridor. Instead of going up, we went through a door I first thought was for service stuff. Another flight of stairs greeted us and we were downstairs, in the basement. He took out his keys and opened the first door to the left and violà, we'd arrived at his bachelor pad.

I don't know why I was suddenly so nervous. After all, I was with Thomas and trusted him completely. This was nothing like the backseat of Aidan's borrowed Volvo. I hadn't had anything to drink. Things were not out of control or going too fast and besides, Thomas's kisses made my sluggish blood race.

His place was tidy and masculine. A couple of glasses sat in the draining board by the sink. His bed was semimade and visible from the living room. He turned on the lights, set to dim, then pulled me into his embrace. He was more controlled now, gentler and very tender. I kind of wanted the other Thomas back, the passionate one who wanted me right there on the golf course, but I knew he was hiding beneath the surface, ready to be unleashed after making sure I was ready.

"Are you sure you're ready?" he whispered, looking deep into my eyes for the least sign of resistance. I wanted to scream, "Yes! Finally!" into his face but thought it might spoil the mood. Instead I nodded demurely and let me tell you, I don't do demure for just anything.

He led me to his bedroom and kissed me again. My mind flashed to our motel room argument and I knew I couldn't go any further without telling him I was sorry. "Thomas," I said, as he pulled my shirt off over my head, "I'm sorry about California. I should have respected you more."

He kissed one exposed shoulder and then the next. "I understand, Colby, you were excited and wanted to save the day."

Uh, hello? Are we talking about the same thing here?

I pushed him away gently. "No, I mean about being intimate in the hotel room. I shouldn't have blurted out my nonvirgin status to try to goad you into putting out. I think it's sweet that you wanted to wait until you were really ready."

Pausing his tender caresses, he said woodenly, "So, you're sorry about the sex fight but not about skipping out to save Sage and Tina all by yourself?"

I backpedaled quickly. "No, no. I'm sorry about all of it. I was reckless and I should have been a better partner to you on every level."

His muscles relaxed beneath my hands after my confession and he started kissing my neck once more. I should have let it go, I should have shut my big fat mouth and not needed to get the last word in, but then I guess I wouldn't be me then, would I?

"You have to admit," I murmured into his ear, kneading his back with my hands, "I did manage to get the girls without any help."

Thomas froze in mid-caress, pulling away from me quickly.

"So you're not sorry you freed Tina and Sage?"

I looked at him in surprise. "I'm sorry I didn't follow orders, but I didn't really need your help, did I? I'm just saying maybe you don't see how far I've come as a Protector, is all."

"How far you've come as a Protector?" he parroted back to me.

"Ye-ah, I did get them safely to Psi Phi House all on my own."

"And you left me stranded in California in the process," he reminded me.

"I know, I know. I said I was sorry for that." He didn't make apologizing very easy, did he?

"And now Tina is dead."

His statement hung in the air.

"Are you implying that if I hadn't freed the half-bloods

on my own then Tina would still be alive?" My voice was dead calm.

"I'm saying if you had followed orders and waited for me, we both would have returned to Psi Phi House together and I might have been able to stop Tina's death."

"*You* might have been able to stop Tina's death? You, all on your own. Because Thomas, God's gift to Vampire Investigators, would have single-handedly saved Tina if *he'd* only been there?!"

I flung myself away from him and grabbed the shirt he'd discarded only moments before. I yanked it over my head and was walking to the door before I'd even managed to get my arms through the holes.

"Where're you going?" he demanded.

I grabbed his keys off the counter, made a very unladylike suggestion of what he could go do and left his apartment.

Eleven

Once outside, I realized that although I'd swiped Thomas's keys, I wasn't about to steal his car. I was awfully tempted though so I dumped the keys in his mail slot and walked down the street. After I was far enough away from his building, I pulled out my cell phone and debated who to call.

Piper was out of town and it was way too late to call my parents. I scrolled down the list of numbers and thought that I should really get a car or something. I paused over Carl's number and after much debate, hit the speed dial. Carl would pick me up with very little questioning. Because he was extremely professional or really didn't want to know, I wasn't sure. I just knew I could count on him and that's what I needed right now. Someone I could count on.

Carl arrived in twenty minutes. His gray Saab perfectly

accented his dark good looks. It's a shame he and Piper didn't go out again after Homecoming, though they seemed quite fond of each other. Dating a vampire was so complicated.

His tinted window rolled down as he pulled up to the curb and said, "Someone call for a pickup from this address?"

I smirked at him and climbed into the car. He might not ask questions but he would make wisecracks the whole way home. At the moment, it was a small price to pay for a lift.

We'd made it safely onto the freeway before he asked, "So, how are you holding up?"

I snorted, my arms crossed as I kept my eyes glued to the side window, as though engrossed in the view.

"O-kay, then," he murmured and we drove the rest of the way in silence.

Once we arrived at Psi Phi House, I felt bad about how I was treating Carl. After all, it wasn't his fault that his partner was an arrogant know-it-all and he had gone out of his way to pick me up. When he parked the car I thanked him for coming to get me.

"Is there something I should know about?" he asked in a concerned way. All of a sudden I needed Carl's take on the situation. I mean, he was here and Tina still died. Did that mean Thomas thought he was incompetent as well? I highly doubted that because he trusted Carl with everything, including Psi Phi House. It was only me that Thomas thought was a bumbling idiot.

"Do you think we could have done something to save Tina, to keep her from dying?"

"Colby, don't beat yourself up about this. Sometimes good people die. You of all people should know that. If we knew something . . ."

"But we did know," I interrupted. "We knew there was a spy somewhere and we didn't stop Tina from being killed."

"Knowing there was a spy who told other vampires where you were going is not the same thing as knowing one of the girls in the house was going to commit murder."

Carl was absolutely right. We didn't know that. No one knew that or Tina might still be here. Thomas wouldn't have done anything differently with the same information we had. It wasn't my fault Tina died because I left Thomas in California.

He was such a friggin' control freak (and I should know 'cause I was Type A as well) that he'd assumed he could have saved Tina had he just been there. Nothing like piling a little pressure on one's self. And Thomas thought I had issues. Hello?! That was certainly the pot calling the kettle black.

"Thanks, Carl, you've really helped me clarify some things."

Carl looked more confused than ever. "Glad I could help. Mind telling me how I enlightened your evening?"

"By making me realize I'm not perfect—"

He raised an eyebrow at my declaration.

"—and neither is anyone else."

My explanation did nothing to alleviate the confused look on his face. I added, "You know, if Piper decides to stay in England you can totally have her job as my best friend."

Carl actually shuddered at my gracious offer. He *shuddered*.

Was being my best friend such a tough gig? I hardly thought so. I decided Vampire Investigators in general had issues to work out.

"Anyway, thanks again."

I climbed out of the car and made my way toward the House. I was nowhere closer to finding the killer than I was before, but now I had something I didn't before. I didn't need to depend on someone else to believe that I'd done my best. That I was a good Protector. I had faith in myself and that was enough for me.

In the house, most of the girls were subdued and hanging out in the basement. The Tribunal had removed Tina's body and everyone seemed to silently agree that upstairs was a no half-blood zone. I tried to comfort them as best I could, but it was difficult because I didn't know if the person I wanted to console was really the killer. In the end, I slipped upstairs to my room and logged onto the Net to check my e-mail.

Awaiting me was a reply from Piper, complaining that she was on vacation and really didn't want to traipse around Ileana's musty old homes but she would do it, of course, as a favor to me, yada, yada, yada. No one did guilt like Piper.

I started to compose a reply and stopped in mid-sentence. How did I announce a half-blood murder in e-mail? Should I ask how her day was first and then say something like, "By the way, you'll never guess what happened to me today"? I lightly tapped my fingers on the keyboard drawer. I should tell her but I didn't want her freaking out that I was in danger.

In the end I decided to forego telling her about Tina but

stressed how important finding out more about Ileana was to me and to start immediately. It sounded sort of melodramatic, even to my ears, but I shrugged. Piper was used to my drama. She wouldn't blink an eye at the tone.

There was a timid knock at my door.

"Come in." I turned off the computer monitor and swung around to greet my guest.

Sage tentatively opened the door and entered.

"Hey," I said gently. "How are you holding up?"

Her eyes were swollen and her skin was blotchy, but despite that she still looked beautiful. Sage was just one of those people.

"I'm doing okay, I guess." She crossed the room. "Can I sit down?"

I jumped to my feet and swept the array of stuffed animals and pillows off my bed. "Of course."

She sat down and looked around my room, eyes settling on a glittering tiara on my dresser.

"Nice crown," she commented.

Not wanting to prompt her if she wasn't ready to speak, I admired the crown as well.

"Homecoming queen, my senior year."

She nodded and admitted, "Your room's cool too."

"Thanks," I responded. Mentally I was poking her with a stick so she would explain why she was here.

"I think I know who killed Tina," she blurted out.

That was so not even in the ballpark of why I thought she was visiting me.

"You do?"

She nodded her head vigorously but said nothing.

"Do you want to tell me who?" I prodded again.

"I . . . I think Lance may have done it."

"Lance? The ex-boyfriend, surfer vampire Lance? What makes you think that?"

"The last time they broke up, I could tell Tina really meant it and so could Lance. They'd broken up before, dozens of times, but Tina was really through with him. Anyway, she told me he took it really hard. He accused her of being ungrateful after all he'd done for her. Then when that tactic didn't work, he told her if he couldn't have her, no one could."

"But we saw Lance arrive with Cookie," I pointed out. Why did vampires have to go off the deep end?

"I thought that too, but when I was talking to Cookie, you know, *after* we found Tina, she mentioned that Lance left the same night we did. He took off right after discovering we'd gone to Psi Phi House. He met Cookie at the airport and brought her here."

I digested this bit of information. I didn't believe that a vampire had broken into the House—but what if Tina invited him in? He could have shown up right before dawn and convinced her to let him inside to talk, and no one would have been the wiser.

But why didn't I see them? I was up at dawn and that was when the Tribunal Security was coming on duty. Could it be I just missed him?

"Thank you for telling me this, Sage. I know how hard all

this is for you. Especially since you trusted me to protect you both."

"I don't blame you, Colby. Cookie begged me to go back with her. She would have gone up against the Tribunal to take me back but I didn't want to go. I want to be here, with others like me. It's like I finally belong, you know?"

Now this reasoning I could totally understand and I was grateful she didn't blame me for Tina's death. If Lance was responsible—and that was still a way big "if" in my mind—there was no safe place for Sage.

"Why didn't you tell Cookie or me sooner, that Lance had threatened Tina?"

Her eyes threatened to overflow again as she answered in a tiny whisper, "Because Tina always exaggerated things. And Lance was sort of the same way, you know? They lived off the drama. I guess I didn't really believe he would hurt her. But I should have, I should have done something."

She broke down into tears again and I rushed to her side.

"Don't. Don't do this to yourself, Sage. You're not to blame. The person who killed Tina is at fault and no one else."

She wiped her nose with a tissue I offered from the desk and nodded in agreement.

"I'm gonna go now. Sophie promised to make some chamomile tea and read Harry Potter to us. It sounds so much cooler when someone with a real English accent reads it."

I hid my surprise that Ileana would let Sophie do anything that wasn't serving her, but then I realized Sophie was probably reading the book to Ileana. And Ileana was just benevolently letting the others stay and listen because Tina had died. She was a saint, that one.

After she left, my computer beeped, telling me I had new mail. It was from Piper.

> C—
> Local vampire lore. Found in book in private library of Ileana's English manor. Got kicked out and missed the changing of the guard to e-mail info to you.
>   —Piper

I stamped down the guilt I felt for intruding on Piper's vacation. Sheesh, it wasn't like she missed something important, like seeing the Crown Jewels or something. It was just a bunch of soldiers getting off work. I tried to tell myself that but I still felt bad. Scrolling down her e-mail, I read the local vampire lore. The whole four sentences of it.

> *This time the mixed blood will rise,*
> *The One who is Undead but Alive,*
> *who is pure but not whole,*
> *And they will bring forth the beginning of the end.*

Huh?

I needed help deciphering this and the only person I could think of was Thomas, but there was no way I was going to ask him for help right now. That left one other person. Ugh, I was going to need a ride, again.

I printed off the e-mail and sought out Carl. He was in the dining room, reviewing documents. How predictable. I stood behind him and started massaging his shoulders.

"How's work coming along, Carl?" I asked sweetly.

"Whatever you want, the answer is no." He didn't even bother to look up from his reading to talk to me.

Twelve

ignored him and continued talking. "Yeah, work can be such a strain. Especially when you don't have a car and need to head to the Tribunal offices to, you know, work."

He continued to ignore me until I pinched his neck.

"Ouch!"

"Sorry, don't know my own strength." I went back to the soothing massage and he went back to ignoring me. After a moment I pinched him again.

"Dammit, get your purse. We'll go right now."

I smiled in satisfaction.

We arrived at the Tribunal offices, Carl grumbling about the cost of gas the entire way.

"I suppose you'll want me to wait for you as well?"

I batted my eyelashes at him in reply. He turned off the

engine, reached into the backseat for his briefcase and followed me inside. Please, it's not like he didn't know that in advance. Why else would he have brought his briefcase?

We rode the elevator up to the top and exited to the plush gray and black offices of the Tribunal. Mrs. Durham sat behind the imposing reception desk, typing away.

"Hiya, Margaret," I greeted her as Carl hid a smile.

She took one look at me and declared, "He's busy."

I nodded enthusiastically, both of my hands on top of the reception desk, which was made of glass. I slid my fingers toward the edges, creating smeared fingerprints on its pristine surface. "Don't I know it? Me too. Busy, busy, busy. But, when you're the *only* half-blood Protector, what's a girl to do?" I shrugged in her direction. Carl settled down in the reception area and pulled some documents out of his case to review. We watched him in silence for a moment. I knew Mrs. Durham was fighting for control so I waited until she gained her composure. I'm not all bad, you know.

"So." I emphasized my point by tapping the glass desk, making more fingerprints. "I'm gonna need to see Mr. Holloway ASAP."

She glared at me, looking from the dirty desktop back up to me, and insisted, "I told you he is very busy."

I blew out my breath and leaned forward. "You know, Margaret, I'm really sorry I missed the shopping excursion. Heard it was memorable. Is that a new outfit you're wearing?" I pretended surprise and delight. "Fabulous color on you. Really, gray is *your* color."

I smiled sweetly, holding her gaze until she finally broke eye contact and grabbed the phone. Her knuckles were white as she announced my presence into the receiver.

I winked at her when I heard Mr. Holloway request she send me back straightaway. Her lips were compressed so tightly, a white ring had formed around them. "He will see you now."

"Great!" I exclaimed. "That's super." I walked toward the side door and heard the buzz indicating she'd unlocked it. I pulled on the handle.

I knew where I was going and walked straight to Mr. Holloway's office. I knocked twice and opened the door. He was seated behind an impressive walnut desk, leaning back in his chair, expecting me.

"Colby," he greeted me. "Must be important if you came all the way down here."

I thought he was scolding me, but chose to ignore the implication that I was wasting his time. Instead I got right to the point and gave him the printed paper with the vampire lore on it.

"What's this?" he asked. Then read the lines. Except for the brief flaring of his nostrils, his face remained impassive.

"At first I thought some vampire clan who hated half-bloods had a spy in the Tribunal and that's how they knew to attack us right after we arrived. But when Tina turned up dead, I started to think it was one of the girls. Sage told me she thought it was Tina's ex-boyfriend." I walked about his office, picking up things, looking them over and then putting them back down.

"I haven't totally written off Lance, gotta talk to him first. But funny thing is, I find out about this little vampire lore and I wonder where it fits in. Why discover it now, in the midst of this mess?"

I ended my speech by sitting in the chair opposite his desk and folding my hands across my chest, elbows supported by the chair arms.

"Colby, where did you get this?" Mr. Holloway finally asked.

"A friend found it for me. What is it, exactly?"

"Vampire myth or lore." He shook the paper gently. "It is difficult to interpret. The ancient texts from which these are translated are dreadfully incomplete. No one knows for sure how much of the original texts exist and who is in possession of them."

"Why is that? Aren't they listed in some vampire library somewhere?"

Mr. Holloway smiled. "You are assuming all the texts reside in one location. That is not the case. Several ancients are collectors, as it were. They alone wish to decipher the texts."

I knew that ancient vampires were a bit fragmented; apparently, they don't share their toys either.

"What do the texts do? Exactly?"

"Do? They foretell the future, for those who put stock in such things."

"Do you? Put stock in such things, that is." I wondered exactly how steeped in political aspirations Mr. Holloway was, or if he still had a little vampire voodoo hunter in him.

"There are some ancient clans who place great stock in the texts. Throughout history, I have even known of human groups who have sought their meaning. It always ends badly. To gather too much information is to make powerful enemies. Perhaps such prophesies are best left undiscovered."

"Do you think Tina discovered something about these texts, or knew too much?" It seemed a far stretch. After all, Tina wasn't the brightest bulb out there.

"Unknown. After talking to Cookie, it seems unlikely. She may have stumbled onto something, quite by accident, that made her a liability. Did you find this in her things?"

"No, Piper found it in a library in one of Ileana's royal houses."

"Ileana Romanav?" He didn't sound terribly surprised.

"Do you think she may have had something to do with Tina's death?"

He shook his head. "No, I wouldn't think so."

I exhaled and slumped back in my chair. Could someone at Psi Phi House be a member of one of these ancient clans who guarded the texts or sought to understand the prophesy? If so, why not Ileana? It was odd Mr. Holloway seemed pretty unconcerned that I'd found the texts in her ancestral home.

"It sounds like this Lance character is a good lead. Even so, we shouldn't rule out a spy in the House. There are clans of vampires who are capable of killing half-bloods and feel they are justifiable in doing so. Their hatred is great and there is no telling what lengths they will go to to end Psi Phi House and the program."

"But not Ileana?" I had no leads and really thought the grand duchess reeked of suspicion.

"No one is above suspicion, Colby. Some think perhaps you killed Tina. That the pressure of being the Protector has become too much and you may have snapped under the pressure."

Gee, I wonder what little bird was whispering *that* into his Tribunal ear? I inadvertently glared at his closed door, wishing I could kill Margaret with a single glance.

"So, no one is above suspicion but some candidates are less likely than others?" I interpreted. Mr. Holloway smiled at me and nodded.

"I have faith in you," he said, handing back the paper, in effect dismissing me.

I stood up and walked to the door. As I did, he said, "I meant what I said about there being vampires who would think it was nothing to kill the members of Psi Phi House. You must be ever vigilant."

I nodded. Even I had a lot to think about. I needed to question Lance and continue to patrol my fellow sisters and perhaps dig a little deeper into Ileana's life, despite Mr. Holloway's doubt she was involved. Playing Investigator was giving me a headache. What I needed was a little snack to boost my energy.

Carl was waiting for me where I left him. When he saw me, he immediately packed up his things and we walked out of the reception area. I remembered what Mr. Holloway said about someone thinking I murdered Tina and offered a cutesy "Toodles, Margaret" as we left.

Once we were safe inside the elevators Carl scolded me, "Colby, we've told you a million times not to provoke that woman but you just don't listen. She is a powerful figure in the Tribunal and not an enemy you want to have."

I didn't want to tell Carl what malicious lies Durham was spreading about me, since he knew she hated me and wouldn't believe her anyway. I just shrugged and changed the subject. "What do you know about vampire lore?"

"Vampire lore? You mean like vampire legends and myths?" I nodded and he said, "As much as the next Undead, I guess. Why do you ask?"

We exited the elevator and made our way through the parking garage to his car. "Do you know of any prophesies that vampires believe in? You know, the way some humans believe the Book of Revelations. Doom, end of the earth, the coming of the apocalypse. Some believed Nostradamus's prophesies. Anything like that for vamps?"

He rubbed his chin a moment and thought. "I'm told ancient vampire texts existed once, but not anymore. The blood wars destroyed a lot of our history, I'm sorry to say. Other than that, I guess we have our version of Nostradamus just like humans but his predictions were more about demons than vampires."

"Demons?" I asked, surprised, as we arrived at his car.

"Well sure, you didn't think we were the only Undead walking the earth, did you? Really Colby, that's kind of arrogant, don't you think?" He slid into the driver's side and I hurried to join him in the car.

"So there are demons walking around, just like there are vampires?"

Carl started the car and maneuvered out of the parking garage. "I'm not sure they hang out in public or anything. They look much different than humans. Vampires can do it because we are so similar to the living."

"Huh," I said, because I didn't have anything else to add. Imagine that.

"What about hard-core full-blood bigots? Know any of them?"

Carl snorted. "Yes, and so do you."

"I do?"

"Yes, and you insist on needling her every time you come to the Tribunal office."

So Margaret was hard-core, was she? Note the utter lack of surprise on my part. At least she didn't just hate me—she hated *all* the girls.

"So where to next?" He seemed to accept the fact that he'd become my unofficial chauffeur for the night.

"Feel like setting a trap?" I asked.

"Are you the bait?" he countered.

"Absolutely."

"Then I'm in."

Thirteen

Yes, Carl could easily take Piper's place if the need ever arose.

I filled him in on the Lance situation, which he insisted on relaying to Thomas. They spoke on the cell phone while I blatantly tried to pretend like I was ignoring the conversation when I was secretly eavesdropping, but I couldn't hear Thomas's end of the conversation at all. Why is it that super hearing was the one vampire trait I didn't get? How fair was that?

Carl hung up and announced that Thomas didn't like our plan for using me as bait to trap Lance.

"So that's that?" I said. "Thomas says no and you go all girly? He's not the boss of me."

Carl smiled at my petulance. "No, but he is the boss of me."

I pouted in silence and after a moment, Carl said, "It's a beautiful night, isn't it?"

I snorted, with my hands folded across my chest, and said, "Whatever."

Carl ignored me and continued. "Yep, you sure don't see nights this nice all the time. The weather is mild, the stars are bright. It's the perfect night for a walk in the park."

I straightened up a bit when I finally caught on to what Carl was insinuating.

"You know, I *was* feeling a little hungry. It would be a shame to waste such a nice evening."

He nodded in my direction. "I could feed."

I nodded to him as well. "Sure, so could I."

We didn't say another thing for the rest of the drive. Carl parked his car in front of Psi Phi House and got out. I scrambled to join him and we both turned toward the university instead of the House.

"You know, Colby," Carl remarked loudly, "I'm worried what a toll this entire Tina thing is having on you. You look positively awful."

I was about to tell him to keep it down, I wasn't deaf, when it occurred to me he was being loud on purpose.

"Uh, oh yeah. I barely have any strength with the stress of this job and all." I winked at him to show him I was on board with the subterfuge but he rolled his eyes at my playacting ability. Well excuse me, I guess I missed drama class on account of I had a life.

We walked down the middle of the street for the few

blocks it took to get to the park. Once we arrived, Carl immediately led me down the tree-covered trail. *Gee, wasn't I attacked here before?* The thought flashed through my mind.

Carl reached his hand out to stop me. I could smell the change in the air and turned to face the direction of the wind. Walking toward us were five vampires, all dressed like they wandered away from the beach and couldn't find their way back.

Each head possessed sun-kissed locks and their shirts were open at the chest. I noted the leader's shorts were OP and I wondered if Lance had been changed in the eighties and just never updated his style. Or maybe he was going for the retro look.

They stopped in front of us, not making a move to attack. Lance was a few steps ahead of the group so I shrugged at Carl and took two steps forward, so we were eye to eye.

"You must be Lance," I said. "I'm very sorry about what happened to Tina."

Lance seemed surprised by my sincerity. Hey, I liked Tina and was sorry she died. I knew Lance loved her, in his own perverted way. If he didn't kill her then he was probably hurting right now.

"You took her away from me."

Though technically that was true, I believe he was implying that if it wasn't for me she would still be dating him. And that was a crock so I said as much.

"Are you mockin' my pain, man?" he asked incredulously.

"No," I reassured him. "But I didn't take Tina away from

you. She left of her own accord. She *wanted* to get away from you. It was what it was."

"I could have convinced her to come back to me if you hadn't taken her away. She always came back to me."

I could see this conversation was getting us nowhere and I had no desire to play counselor to a whacked-out vampire about the intentions of his dead ex-girlfriend.

"Did you kill her because she left?" I said bluntly.

He seemed shocked I could even voice such a sentiment.

"Hurt my little angelfish? Harsh, dude. She was my sunshine girl."

The vampires behind him nodded in agreement. They whispered to one another. The consensus of his posse seemed to be that Lance would never hurt Tina. He *loved* her, man. Really loved her.

"Okay, well, the Tribunal thinks that maybe you had a hand in her death, so why don't you come with us and we'll go downtown and straighten this whole misunderstanding out."

I couldn't believe I just used the phrase "we'll go downtown and straighten this whole misunderstanding out." What was I, on a rerun of *Law & Order*?

"I'm not going anywhere with you. You're the reason Tina is dead."

His buddies nodded in agreement.

This so wasn't going the way I hoped. I looked to Carl for help but he didn't take his eyes off of Lance for a moment. I wondered if we were going to have to take Lance by force, but they slowly started to back away.

"We'll meet again, blond girl, and when we do, you'll pay for what happened to my angelfish."

Suddenly, they were gone. I looked to Carl: Should we chase them? But Carl stood immobile. Which was just as well, I really didn't want to chase a bunch of surfers through the park. The thought alone exhausted me.

"I don't think he did it," Carl remarked.

I nodded in agreement. The guy was obviously unstable and hopelessly out of fashion but I didn't think he offed Tina either. Which led us back to the spy-among-us theory. And that really sucked.

Carl walked me back to the house after we fed. The Lance encounter weighed heavily on both of us. Sure, we didn't think he killed Tina but he promised to make me pay for her death so I had yet another stress to add to my growing list.

It was close to morning when I said good night to Carl, who was camping out in the housemother's room (can you say, ewww?). On the upside, I didn't think our spy would try anything with a Vampire Investigator in the house so that was somewhat of a relief.

I climbed up the stairs and went to my room. There was no sign of Sophie sleeping in front of Ileana's door so either she was inside the room now or hadn't retired yet. I was wondering how the Harry Potter reading had gone when I entered my bedroom and noticed the flashing light of my answering machine blinking.

Caller ID assured me that I did indeed know who left me a message and I opted to ignore it. It was Thomas and I didn't want to deal with our issues right now. I couldn't even get a grasp of the House issues. Instead I turned off my cell phone as well and changed into my sushi pajamas. Then I curled up in a ball to sleep.

*   *   *

I managed to keep everyone alive and avoid Thomas for five whole days. On the fifth day I awoke to the insistent ringing of my phone. The clock told me it was two in the afternoon, so I knew it couldn't be Thomas.

"Hello?"

"Hi honey, Mom here."

"Mom, do you have any idea what time it is?"

"Of course I do. It's two in the afternoon."

"That's like two in the morning, vampire time, Mom." Why couldn't she remember I slept during the day? "Everyone's okay, right? Aunt Chloe? Dad?"

"Everyone's fine, dear. I'm sorry I woke you. I never know when you're sleeping. Anyway, we thought we would come over tonight and take you out to dinner. Well, we'd eat and you could fill us in about your first week with your new roommates."

I made a face at the phone. Yeah, that sounded like a great time. So Mom, someone is trying to kill us and has succeeded once. Oh and by the way, the killer lives in the house. Yeah, not a conversation I was having with my family.

"You know, Mom, that sounds great but we're kind of vampire testing here. Maybe I could swing by after training?"

"Oh, that might work."

"Great, but don't wait for me to have dinner. I'm not sure how long I can stay."

We gossiped a bit more and then she rang off. I missed my mom, but I couldn't have my family anywhere near Psi Phi House until the killer was caught.

I looked at the clock and groaned when I remembered Cyrus would be waiting for me at 4 P.M. to train. I debated calling him and canceling but knew I should go. I was going to enlist Cyrus to help train the other girls as well. But first I needed to catch the killer. No use training *her* to be a better fighter. Until then, I needed all the advanced training I could get.

I threw on yoga pants and a cheer shirt. I slathered on sunscreen and made my way downstairs. I decided to peek into the rec room and found Lucy on the computer, checking her e-mail. She was alone in the room.

"Surprised to see you up," I said. She didn't start so I assumed she heard me coming. Guess I was not the most silent Undead in the house. She quickly minimized her screen and turned toward me.

"You on e-mail?" I asked.

"Uh, yeah. Is that okay?"

"Sure, sure. I think it's great you have friends to keep in touch with, now that, well you know." I was surprised that she corresponded so much. I'd gotten the impression she was all alone but she was always on the computer. It was great she had support, even if it was electronically offered.

"I'm having a hard time sleeping, ya know? Thought

catching up with my old friends via e-mail might make me feel better."

I nodded. "Everyone else asleep?" I motioned toward the dorm room.

She shrugged. "The rest of the gals are probably still upstairs. Sophie's been reading us Harry Potter and everyone thought it would be a good idea to sleep in the same room. Just in case."

"But you couldn't sleep?" I prodded.

Lucy looked around in a conspiring sort of way and finally admitted, "Ileana snores like no one I've ever met. I thought Sophie was crazy to sleep outside her door in the hallway but now I know why: It's probably the only way she can get a decent night's rest!"

I laughed and was immensely pleased with the idea that Ileana, our English lady and resident pain in the backside, snored like a sailor.

"Well, I'm off to meet someone who might be able to start training you gals in self-defense. Remember that Carl is here and the Tribunal Security is outside. You guys should be just fine."

She nodded to me in an absentminded way, then stifled a yawn. "I think I'll try to sleep again."

"Headed upstairs?" I asked.

"No way, I'm going straight to the dorm room, where it's nice and quiet."

I laughed as she headed off to bed and made my way upstairs. I left a note for Carl and stepped out onto the porch.

Zach was again guarding the porch and I was relieved that Todd was nowhere in sight.

"I'm off to the bus stop," I told him.

"Great, that's a pretty short walk."

"It is a short walk, you really don't have to . . ."

He waved my statement away. "All part of the Security gig."

It only took a couple of minutes to make our way to the major bus stop outside PSU. In as few as three bus transfers and almost two hours of travel, I finally made it to Cyrus's studio.

"You're late," he said flatly.

"Dude, don't even start with me. I've been riding public transportation for two hours to get here. And I'm so not happy about it."

"When are you going to get a car?" he asked.

"On my list, on my list," I assured him, going straight into stretches.

We began our workout with forms and then advanced to a little sparring. "I have a little surprise for you," he said as he ushered me into the back room.

I followed, intrigued by the surprise. When I found myself in a musty storage room that doubled as his office, I was more than a little disappointed.

"So what's the surprise? You want me to do your books?"

He smirked. "Hardly. Today we're going to do a little improvisation. After you failed my surprise attack so dismally last week"—he cast a disapproving gaze in my direction—"I thought we definitely needed to work on some real world situations."

"Okay. So why are we here?"

"I'm going to attack you and you're going to defend yourself using everyday objects found in my office."

"Wait a second, I don't want to break anything . . ." I started to complain but he attacked me swiftly and I staggered back from the force of a blow to my face.

Fourteen

stopped worrying about his stuff and engaged in combat. A real fight takes very little time. In actuality, it should take only a few moves. The object is to win by any means necessary and in the shortest amount of time. The problem with sparring with the same partner is we knew each other pretty well and it became like a dance. We could counter each other's moves and look really cool doing it.

However, Cyrus was regretting our complacency and was now determined to remedy the situation.

"Pretend I'm a vampire, find a weapon against me," he panted, avoiding my roundhouse kick.

I grabbed the letter opener from the desk and jabbed at his face. He punched my arm to the side and whipped me around, grabbing me from behind in a sleeper hold.

"A knife?! You're gonna attack a vampire with a knife? Get your head in the game, girlie."

I stomped on his instep and butted my head back forcefully, connecting with his nose. He released me in surprise and I turned to face him again. His nose was bleeding but neither of us stopped our aggression, though it made my stomach growl.

I attacked again, but this time he used my momentum to fling me across the desk, scattering paperwork and desktop minutiae everywhere.

He grabbed me by the hair and lifted me up from the floor. I punched at his chest and said, "I win."

My fist stayed in contact with his chest as he asked, "How do you figure?"

I pulled back the clenched hand and opened it to reveal a regular yellow #2 pencil. I'd grabbed it from the desk when he threw me. I could have imbedded it into his heart if I'd turned my fist appropriately.

The look of shock on his face was rewarding. Yeah baby, I beat you. Give it up for Colby Ninja Master, using office supplies to defend half-bloods, one pencil at a time.

"Are you sure that would work? Aren't you supposed to use a stake?" He was skeptical at best.

"Wood in the heart is all it takes. This little baby would have done the job," I assured him cockily.

"Okay then, well done. Now get me some ice for my nose from the food mart next door."

Cyrus's studio was located in a mini mall on the eastside. I filled a glass with ice and after paying full soda price for it (can you believe that?), I quickly returned to him. He wrapped the ice in a towel and balanced it on the bridge of his nose while leaning back in his chair.

"So, I have a proposal for you. I was thinking you might want to start teaching the girls self-defense."

"And why do you think I would want to do that?" he asked in a muffled voice.

"Because I'll pay you," I enticed sneakily.

"Pay me what? You're a poor mutant Undead. What are you offering? An exchange of cheerleading lessons for self-defense classes?" He tried to chuckle at his little joke, but groaned in pain after the first snort.

"Hardly. The Tribunal will pay, of course. Just get me a quote for biweekly defense lessons for four newbies."

"I thought you had five girls at the house," he countered.

I walked to the studio door, turned back and said, "Did I mention how unpopular half-blood vampires are?"

He removed the ice from his nose and looked at me. "Be careful," he warned.

I nodded and walked out of his office. As I reached the front door he yelled, "Next week, Tuesday and Thursday evenings. Eleven P.M. Tell the girls not to be late."

I called my mom to pick me up from the studio and passed the time reading the magazines in the food mart. The nice Indian man behind the counter glowered at me but what could he really say? I'd purchased ice earlier so I was a paying customer, right?

Mom was pretty happy to see me and I was excited to visit

with the family for awhile. We chatted, they ate, but I couldn't stay too long or I would miss my bus back to Seattle.

"Why not stay the night here?" Aunt Chloe asked.

I turned to my great-aunt and marveled that such a strong, steady voice came from such a tiny, frail-looking woman.

"And do what? Mom and Dad will be going to bed soon. They have to work tomorrow."

"You could talk to me. I don't need as much sleep as those two. I'm pretty much a night owl."

I leaned down and gave her a big hug. "I would love to, Aunt Chloe, but I don't want to miss my bus. A lot of stuff happening at Psi Phi House, you know."

"Hmmph," she snorted. "No, I wouldn't know because my niece has not seen fit to invite me." She crossed her bony arms and glared at me with disapproval.

"Aunt-ie," I whined, "I told you now wasn't a good time. We have vampire testing all week. Maybe once college classes start, I can give you a tour."

She looked at me and I could swear I saw the wheels turning in her curly gray head. She wasn't buying my vampire classes for a minute. She was way too sharp.

"Anyway, I've gotta run. 'Bye Mom, 'bye Dad," I called as I rushed to the door, desperate to get away from the all-knowing Aunt Chloe.

"At least let me give you a ride back to school," Dad offered again.

"Dad, public transportation is the key to saving our environment."

"I see. So if I were to offer you a car, you would turn it down. You know, for the environment?"

"Well, that depends. Are you really offering me a car or giving a hypothetical example?"

He chuckled and hugged me good-bye. Darn, so close. I really did need a car.

I headed toward the bus stop outside of my old school, confidently walking on the trail where I'd once been attacked and changed into the Undead. No reports of rogue vampires in the area and really, what more could happen to me? I was already a half-blood.

It was after dusk when I finally arrived back at Psi Phi House and I was exhausted. All that walking, working out and not getting enough sleep was taking its toll on me. I just wanted to crash.

I groaned when I saw Thomas's car in the driveway. No, I so didn't want to do this right now. I tiptoed around the house to see if the back door was open so I could sneak past him. It was bolted tight, as were all the windows.

I took stock of my options. I could try to scale the house and sneak into my upstairs room. I looked up and shook my head. So not gonna happen. I could cause a distraction outside and when they rushed out to investigate, sneak past them into the house. Oh sure, not a problem. Sneak past two Vampire Investigators. Of course I could. Not.

Finally, I pulled out my cell phone, turned it back on and dialed Carl.

"Carl here," he answered.

"Groovy, good to know. Listen, is there any way you could have an impromptu Investigator party downstairs in the rec room for a minute?"

"Where are you?" he asked and then I heard him say in a muffled voice, "Tribunal Security check-in." At least Carl wasn't going to rat me out to his boss. Aka my boyfriend.

"I'm outside Psi Phi House. I want to sneak up to my room without Thomas seeing me."

"I see," he answered. "That's a good plan. It's best to be safe under the circumstances."

"Ohh, aren't you the covert James Bond? I'll wait five minutes, and then I'll come in through the front door."

I hung up and watched the digital clock on my cell phone turn. Talk about a hopping night. I was literally watching time go past on the face of my cell phone. My life didn't suck, no siree.

I opened the door slowly and peeked inside. The coast looked clear. I scurried across the floor toward the staircase and right when I thought I was home free, a voice from behind me said.

"Do we have to go over the traits of vampires again? Such as strength, excellent eyesight and oh yeah, super hearing?"

Thomas was lying on the couch, completely hidden from the view of the front door.

Fifteen

"Where's Carl?" I asked.

"Downstairs. In a time-out of sorts." He sat up.

"Ha ha. Well, I sure am bushed. Gonna run upstairs, take a shower and take a nap." I turned to leave again.

"Colby, we need to talk," he started.

"Nope, we really don't. What I need is some rest and you need, well, you need to get a clue." And with that, I stalked up the stairs with flourish. Ha, take that, Mr. Vampire Investigator Control Freak.

I walked to my room and heard the lilting English tones of Sophie reading from Harry Potter. *Oh give it a rest already,* I thought grumpily.

I skipped the shower and fell into bed. I'm sure I smelled gamey after my workout with Cyrus but I didn't care. I just wanted to sleep and escape the responsibility of being Protector and the complexity of my relationship with Thomas.

My cell phone rang and I checked the number. Grimacing, I turned the phone off again. Thomas was not giving up.

Several hours later I awoke, not at all refreshed and even more tired than before. I dragged myself to the showers and hoped the hot spray would liven me up a bit. After a long scrubbing, I felt almost human and went to get dressed. Cutoff shorts and a halter top seemed to perk me up. I checked my e-mail and discovered Piper had sent not one, not two, but three missives, all with little red exclamation points next to them. I checked them in order.

> Colby—
> Something is way wrong with Ileana's story, I'm checking
> out two other manors and another private library. Contact you
> when I know more.
> —Piper

Well, that told me nothing. Hardly seemed worth an exclamation point, but then Piper always thought everything she said was interjection worthy. The next message was just as puzzling.

> C—
> Almost have it figured out. They all look the same. Freaky
> stuff here.
> —P

Uh, okay.

The final e-mail cleared everything up and had me sitting up at attention.

> Colby—
>
> Ileana is actually her ancestors. She has been posing as the most recent generation of each Romanav for the last 5 generations. She has masqueraded as her mother, grandmother, great-grandmother and great-great-grandmother. I have attached all their portraits. They are definitely the same person. They are Ileana. Check out the names. They are all hers.
>
> Also, I discovered a journal in the private library of Ileana's father. He belonged to a secret society who worshipped ancient vampires. The purest bloods. Ileana is a vampire! She must be the one! Be careful!!
>
> —Piper

I opened the attachments and sure enough, each portrait was Ileana. My Ileana. I couldn't believe it.

I rushed downstairs to find Thomas or Carl, but neither was around. I finally found Carl, Angie, Sage and Lucy watching a TiVo'd episode of *The O.C.* with Carl interrupting and asking questions.

"So those two used to date but they don't anymore? And she killed some guy?" He seemed confused.

I interrupted them with style. "Ohmigod Ileana is the killer! Where's Thomas? Where's Thomas?"

Yep, I'm one cool cucumber under pressure.

They all started speaking at once.

"What?"

"Ileana is the killer?"

"How do you know?"

Carl took control and calmly asked me to share what information I knew. I told him about Piper's e-mail and asked where Ileana was.

"She went out to feed with Sophie," Lucy said.

"And Thomas escorted them," Angie clarified.

"Oh no!" I cried. "I've got to warn him."

"No," Carl commanded. "Your job is to protect the half-bloods. You're staying here. I'll go to Thomas."

We all followed him upstairs to the front door. He tried to reach Thomas on his cell phone and I jumped when I heard it ring from the living room sofa. Sage rushed over and pulled it out from between the sofa cushions. It must have fallen out of his pocket when he was lying in wait for me.

"Carl," I said in anguish.

"It'll be all right, Colby. I'll find him, I swear." And he rushed out into the night.

Sage started to cry and Lucy hurried to her side and gave her a comforting hug. They sat down on the couch and Lucy stroked her hair, saying everything was going to be just fine.

I turned to go up the stairs and Angie followed.

"Where are you going?" she asked.

"To reread Piper's e-mail."

She followed me to my room and I read the e-mails to her. We sat in shock, coming to grips with the fact that Thomas had left to escort Ileana and she was the spy among us.

"I can't believe it was her," Angie said. "I mean, she was snooty and all but she didn't seem like a killer to me."

I nodded in silent agreement. She was such an obvious choice that I felt sure she was too obvious. She barely held her distaste for all of us in check but after talking to Mr. Holloway, I hadn't really believed she wanted us dead or anything. I thought she was just a snob. And how stupid was it to put Tina in her own trunk anyway? Did she plan to cart it back to England with her? Ick.

"You know how I feel about Tribunal Security but I have to say, I'm glad they're here. Poor Thomas. Imagine if one of *us* had gone to feed with her," Angie admitted.

I remembered how the security force treated Angie upon her arrival and had to admit, I wouldn't have warm and fuzzy thoughts about them either. I couldn't think about Thomas alone with Ileana; it was too painful.

"I imagine Lucy hates them more than you," I offered, standing up, beginning to pace.

Angie snorted. "Puh-lease. They handled her with kid gloves compared to how I was treated. All cops are the same."

"What do you mean? You both arrived tied up and gagged. She was in their care a lot longer than you were."

"They kept me locked up for two weeks! Those guys always treat Latinos the same. Smack us around just for the fun of it. When they took me into the van, they shoved me in so hard I thought I'd black out. When we stopped to pick her up, they gently placed her in the back, careful not to hurt her. She was never locked up with me. I bet they kept her at a Marriott or something."

I froze in place, looking at Angie in horror. Sure the beatings were a shock but you only had to spend a small amount of time in her company to realize she probably goaded them into it. There were times when I felt like smacking her myself and it was my job to protect her.

Something she just said struck a chord with me. "You say she arrived *after* you. That you picked her up on the way to Psi Phi House?"

Angie seemed oblivious to my frame of mind; she was too busy looking at herself in the full-length mirror and rearranging her abundant cleavage barely contained in a tiny tank top.

"Yep."

I tried to remember back to the night Angie and Lucy arrived at Psi Phi House.

"I can't explain it myself. After I was attacked and changed, I was taken away to a place I can only describe as a kind of prison. They fed me and let me watch TV and stuff but I was there all alone for months before Angie joined me and then we were transported here."

Lucy had said she was captured and placed in a holding cell until Angie joined her. Angie just told me they picked up Lucy on the way to Psi Phi House. What was going on here?

I thought back to every conversation I had with Lucy. She told me she had no one and yet admitted to e-mailing friends just last night. When we were jumped by two vampires in the park, she conveniently disappeared. At the time I thought it was self-preservation, but what if she planned it all along? She was the one who came to me that night. She was the one who suggested feeding. Ohmigosh, I was an idiot!

"Angie," I said quietly, "get out of the house and go find Security. Don't stop, no matter what, just go."

Sixteen

She froze at the tone in my voice, eyes wide with surprise. I pulled open the door and made my way down the hallway. When Angie and I went upstairs, Lucy was consoling Sage.

I stepped down onto the main floor and caught a glimpse of Lucy bending over Sage, pulling a throw blanket up to her chin. She appeared to be sleeping.

Lucy must have heard us coming because she turned quickly, placed a finger to her lips and shushed us.

"She's worn out, poor thing. I'm going to get some more tea." She straightened with a small smile and crossed our path on the way to the kitchen. I watched her warily and stepped down into the living room.

Angie made for the door but slowed down as she passed the living room couch. I watched in dread as she crept closer to Sage and pulled back the blanket. Angie gasped, biting back a shriek when she saw the fang marks on Sage's neck.

"Angie, get out of here!" I hissed and ducked down the hall. If Lucy was in the kitchen I would surprise her by coming in the other way, giving Angie time to escape. I snuck as quickly as I could and crouched down to peek around the corner. I was greeted by a swift kick in the face.

Down I went, flying backward into the entryway of the library. Note to self: Do not crouch when peeking into a room to spy on a half-blood assassin. Oh yeah, and getting kicked in the face by a person wearing pink bunny slippers hurts more than you'd think.

Lucy stood in the kitchen doorway leaning against the jam.

"I really should thank you, Colby, for all those little bull sessions getting to know each other in the recreation room." She advanced toward me.

"How else would I know the full extent of everyone's abilities? You're just too helpful." She emphasized her last statement with another kick. This time to my stomach.

"Ooof!" I grunted, scrambling back into the library to give myself room to get up. I tried to do a quick roll from my back to my feet but the pain in my gut made the move difficult. I ended up turning on my side and crawling to my knees to stand.

She seemed in no hurry and not the least bit tired, which was more annoying than anything. She just wanted to chat while kicking my ass.

"So you're the spy," I spat out, stating the obvious. Can I come up with the snappy one-liners in a crisis or what?

Her voice tinkled like a musical bell when she laughed. How could evil sound so darn cute? "There is no spy, you idiot. There never was any full-blood vampire conspiracy to end the existence of half-bloods." She smirked at the thought and I got a good look at crazy. Yep, she was sooo not sane.

"Then why kill Tina?"

"Tina? That little snoop was reading my e-mail! I wasn't going to let her ruin everything I'd worked so hard to accomplish."

"Then why send your goons after us in the park?" I asked, backing up slowly to the hidden door.

"My goons? Are you kidding? Those were actually a couple of vampires who were looking for a legitimate meal. They figured out what you were by your scent."

I knew it!! We *did* smell different.

"And Colby." I stopped at the tone in her voice. "Do you really think I don't remember where the hidden staircase is?" She tipped her head to one side and gave me a pitying look. Well, duh, for a second I felt pretty stupid. Of course she knew what I was trying to do.

I gave her a self-deprecating smile and launched myself straight at her, catching her off guard. If anyone asked, I *meant* to fool her with the door thing and attack her. You know, if anyone asked.

We went flying backward into the hallway again and she neatly tossed me over her head and I crashed into the lower cabinets of the kitchen island. Man, she was strong. Way stronger than any half-blood . . .

"Hey! You're a vampire," I accused, struggling to right myself and hide behind the island.

"Gee," she said, cocking her head to one side again, "look who just caught up."

I scrambled around, desperate for a weapon, but the best I could find were the kitchen knives on the counter. Sure, I had gourmet knives galore stocked in our kitchen to keep up appearances but what I really needed was a wooden stake.

I eyed the set of Kyocera knives and grabbed the one with the largest handle. I was at the end of the island and stood up with the blade between my fingers. Lucy took one look at me and laughed again.

"I can't believe you, the Protector, the one who is foretold to bring upon the end of the world as we know it, is going to fight another vampire *with a knife*."

I backed away until I was in the dining room and she cleared the island.

"Don't come any closer," I warned her and she put her hands on her hips, copping an attitude.

"Or you'll what?" she mocked.

I threw the knife swiftly and it embedded in her chest. She looked down at the handle, sighing heavily. "Col-by, you already know I can't be killed with a blade."

I leapt forward and spun around, kicking my leg out into the knife protruding from her chest with all the force I could muster. She flew back over the top of the island, a look of shock on her face when she saw the handle of the knife flush with her skin. No, the blade couldn't kill her, but the wooden handle could.

"Who said anything about the blade?" I panted softly.

Yeah, I might have overlooked stocking the kitchen with old-fashioned stakes, but I had a boatload of wood-handled knives. Only the best for Psi Phi House.

She slid to the floor, eyes wide with surprise. Even in death she couldn't believe I'd beaten her. I turned around in time to see a bloodied and battered Thomas witness my triumph. He was being helped through the door by Angie and Sophie.

"What happened?" I gasped, rushing to Thomas's side.

"I'm fine. I'm good. Never better," he insisted, trying to stand on his own. Sophie quickly grabbed a dining room chair for him and he sank gratefully down.

"Ileana did this?" I asked, more confused than anything else.

"My lady could never do such a thing!" Sophie protested hotly.

"They were jumped, by Lance and his buddies," Angie clarified. So Tina's rejected lover had stayed around to seek revenge after all. Well, he was nothing if not persistent.

"Then where's Ileana?" I wondered if she'd escaped the entire skirmish by hiding in the bushes, not willing to dirty her clothes and fight.

"She kicked their asses, Colby!" Angie exclaimed, full of awe and pride. "You should have seen it. I never knew she could do all that martial arts stuff. For a skinny English chick she has some mad skills."

"Well, I would certainly hope that after one hundred years of existence, my lady would have picked up a thing or two," Sophie announced stiffly, her back straight with indignation.

"Thomas?" I prodded.

"It seems Piper was half-right. Ileana Margaret Mary Mircea Romanav is her mother Ileana, her grandmother Margaret, her great-grandmother Mary and her great-great-grandmother Mircea all rolled into one. But she's still just a half-blood."

"I don't understand. She's been pretending all these years and switching identities after each generation? Why all the deceit? Why not just tell us?"

"As if she could, mum." Sophie rushed to Ileana's defense. "Back home she'd have been tortured and ripped apart. It isn't all civilized in England like it is here in America. She had no idea if she could trust you. And who could blame her? She's been hiding her true identity going on five generations. But I knew the truth." She puffed up with pride. "It's my family's legacy. Passed down from mother to daughter, to serve my lady and keep her secret. To protect her from harm."

That explained the dog-like devotion to her boss. Suddenly Ileana walked through the door, vainly attempting to brush off the grass stains from her capri pants.

"Sophie, you'll never be able to get these stains out! It's a travesty. The Tribunal will just have to take us on another shopping trip. How many clothes have I ruined since arriving at this, this shoe box? Two, three pairs of trousers? Well, enough already . . ." She lost steam when she caught sight of Lucy across the kitchen.

"Did she try to kill someone else?"

I gasped.

"Well really, who else could it be? Oh yes, you thought I was the mole." She shook her head and rolled her eyes. "Keeping you people from harm has simply exhausted me. Do you have any idea how hard it was making sure none of you were ever alone with her?"

She walked to the kitchen faucet and clucked her tongue while filling a glass with tap water. "It's a wonder I don't look my age." She took a sip.

I stood with my mouth hanging open until a moan from the couch caught my attention.

"Sage," I said and rushed to her side.

She was pale. Okay, she was always pale. I meant she was pale*r* than normal and very weak but she was awake. Lucy simply didn't have enough time to completely drain her.

"You're okay." I showed my relief by pulling her into my arms for a hug.

"My, my, my. I'm gone for one week and I catch you in the arms of another woman."

I turned in surprise as Piper strolled through the door with Carl right behind her.

"What are you doing back so soon?"

She looked around the room, noting Thomas's condition

and Lucy in the kitchen. "Apparently missing all the fun, it would seem. Are you okay?"

I felt tears fill my eyes. Piper came home because she was worried about me. My e-mail must have tipped her off that something was terribly wrong and she couldn't stay in England knowing I was facing danger alone.

"You came home because of my e-mail." I smiled brightly through the tears.

"Uh, no. I came home after Thomas called me. Your e-mail was pretty demanding and not a little annoying."

I glanced over at Thomas, who suddenly found a spot on the carpet so fascinating he couldn't seem to look away from it.

"Thomas." I used my warning tone.

"Okay, I tracked down Piper in Europe. I was at my wit's end, Colby. You wouldn't talk to me. You certainly wouldn't listen to me and you were in grave danger."

"So you called my best friend to what? Straighten me out?" I asked incredulous.

Piper took this moment to intervene. She waved her hand as though trying to clear the air. "No, no. It wasn't like that at all. He called me to get more details about Ileana and when he told me you weren't listening to him I asked what he'd done wrong. So he told me and I *straightened him out*."

I looked questioningly at Thomas, who nodded in agreement. "She really did."

At this point Sophie cleared her throat and suggested Ileana, Angie and Sage head upstairs to clean up after their ordeal. Piper took the hint and followed Ileana, peppering her with questions. Carl pulled out his cell phone and called the Tribunal to arrange pickup for Lucy's body, leaving Thomas and me alone in the living room.

He stood up, painfully slow and grimacing the entire time, and made his way over to me on the couch. I tried not to wince when I saw how injured he was but a tiny part of me watched his progress with satisfaction. He'd taken a beating by some California vampires, and surfer vampires at that. I'd managed to terminate Lucy without much casualty. Of course, she was a crazy, lone vampire, but still. It was something.

"So, who kicked your butt?" I teased and he smiled through a cut lip.

"We were jumped by five vamps. Ileana and Sophie took on Lance while the others were focused on me."

"Must be that new cologne you're wearing," I quipped smartly, gently sweeping his hair off his bloodied forehead.

"No less than I deserve," he admitted, causing my hand to still a moment.

"How do you figure?"

He stopped my hand and tucked it into this. "Colby, you were right."

His admission filled my head and I almost felt dizzy with the power of the moment. So much so that I pretended to swoon on the couch.

He gave my hand a swift tug. "Very funny."

"I'm just so, so very *shocked*, is all."

He nodded toward me. "I deserve that. I just couldn't see things clearly. You're not the girl I met a year ago. Scared, shallow, self-centered . . ."

"Whoa there, stud, so not helping your case here," I warned him dryly.

"What I mean is that you've changed. No, not changed really. You had the skills all along. You've just . . ." He struggled to find the right words but he didn't need to. I understood what he meant.

I leaned forward and touched my forehead to his. "Thank you."

He smiled deeply, the dimple I loved flashed and my heart surged.

"You're a good Protector, Colby. The best. No one, including me, could do it better. Tina wasn't your fault."

I knew that but I was swelling with pride because now Thomas recognized it as well. I didn't need his approval or his acceptance but it was wonderful to have all the same.

"You know, we should probably check you out from head to toe. Make sure there aren't any serious injuries hiding beneath all those clothes."

"Hmmm, you could be right. I wouldn't want to risk a serious internal injury by being neglectful."

I stood up slowly and gently pulled him to his feet. His hand still in mine, I guided him up the stairs to my bedroom. "It's always better to be safe than sorry."

Thomas smiled shyly. "Colby? Do you still have that purple bikini?"

Seventeen

After several hours of close scrutiny and one swimwear fashion show later I declared Thomas fit as a fiddle. We left my room and walked down the stairs. I wondered aloud, "I bet Margaret is the inside guy at the Tribunal."

"Colby! Do you have any proof?" Thomas was shocked.

"Well, none other than the fact that she hates me. But you have to admit, it's fishy. She's a known bigot and she's in a position of power. Aren't you always telling me not to provoke her because she would be a powerful enemy?"

I led him down the stairs.

"I meant she could screw up your paperwork and get you in hot water with Holloway, not she would try to use her connections to have you killed," he said, exasperated.

"Oh." I was a bit disappointed by his confession. "I still

think she's up to something." She *had* screwed up my paper-work in the summer and told Mr. Holloway she thought I killed Tina. She was far more dangerous than Thomas suspected.

We stepped onto the main landing and headed around the stairs to make our way to the library.

"Well, that may be, but you can't go around accusing her without any proof. Anyway, who says Lucy didn't bribe Tribunal Security or hypnotize them?"

"Hmmph."

We opened the secret door and I said saucily, "You know, you were much more agreeable upstairs."

We joined the rest of the house in the recreation room.

"I still don't understand why Lucy killed Tina," Sage said.

"Probably read her e-mails online," Ileana said to no one in particular, as she painted her toenails.

"How'd you know?" I said.

"Tina used the same computer Lucy did the day she was killed. I suspect Lucy never logged off her e-mail account. You can just click through the history tab and go right back into the mail if it's still the same day and you don't log out first."

She looked up at our shocked faces.

"What? You think since I live in England in a family manor I don't have broadband or know how to use a computer? Tina always looked at everyone's history cache. She was nosy. It's how I figured out Lucy was the killer. Not that any of you bothered to use deductive reasoning."

Ileana turned to Sage and said, "I'm sorry, I know you two were close and all, but she was nosy."

Sage nodded slowly, "Yes, she was. And she had the worst habit of borrowing my clothes without asking. Even so, I do miss her. Our summer together was one of the best."

I looked at her, surprised. "Just one summer? This summer?"

"Oh yeah, remember she said she wished she could be a vampire and it came true? Lance was really hot for her and kept hounding her. She'd blow hot and then cold. She really couldn't decide how she felt about him. Finally she refused to come out of her room at night, would only be up during the day so she didn't have to see him."

"And Cookie was okay with this?"

"She wasn't thrilled, but she still had me to keep the party going. She loved Tina and only wanted her to be happy. Remember, at this time Tina wasn't Undead yet. She knew about all of us but she didn't care. Cookie took her in out of the kindness of her heart. Tina really wasn't cut out for the vampire life, being vegan and all."

"What about Lance?" Piper prompted.

"Yeah, anyway, he finally managed to get Tina to go for a walk on the beach with him and he changed her. Cookie was pissed. I'd never seen her so angry before. But when Tina woke up, she was so happy. It was really weird. I think she glamorized the whole vampire thing in her head."

We all nodded and Angie asked, "What happened to you, Sage? Why did Cookie turn you and not want to turn Tina?"

"I'd made my way from Iowa to California to see the ocean. I always wanted to see the ocean before I died. I was diagnosed with leukemia. With about six weeks to live, I was walking on the beach outside her house the evening when we met. She came out of the house to enjoy the ocean mist when she saw me kicking up the surf.

"We chatted and she turned me that night. She knew she couldn't make full-bloods and explained how it would be for me. I certainly didn't want to die but I wonder if I made the right choice sometimes."

"Of course you did," Sophie interjected, "if you don't mind me saying so, mum. Eternal life in exchange for no life seems like more than a fair exchange."

Every half-blood exchanged looks with the others, keeping our opinion to ourselves. Sophie would never know what it was like to be a half-blood, though she dedicated her life to serving one. It was not a life filled with glory or power. It possessed its own set of miseries and shortcomings but still, I was happy Sage was with us. Glad I wasn't alone anymore.

"What was the deal with the crazy vampire lore I sent you, anyway?" Piper spoke up, while we were lost in thought.

"Ohmigosh, the prophesy!" I couldn't believe I hadn't thought of it before.

I went to the computer I last saw Lucy using, checked the history cache as Ileana suggested and found the site I was looking for. I clicked on the link. User had logged out. Crap! Apparently Lucy learned her lesson. I clicked on a couple of other links and found a board site requiring user ID but could still access the first page. It was a reader board for some group calling themselves The Prophet Seekers.

Piper was reading over my shoulder. "Looks like Lucy belonged to a vampire clan led by some ancient full-blood who's collecting vampire texts. This ancient claims to have a bunch of texts similar to the lore I found." Piper looked at me and added, "Other than the lore from Ileana's home, we still have no idea what other texts say implying you're the one."

"Only the looniest of vamps believes that silly lore. To think Colby is the prophesied one who could end vampire existence? Quite ridiculous, really," Ileana scoffed.

"Why ridiculous?" I demanded. Hey, I could destroy vampire existence if I put my mind to it. Well, I could.

"Oh Colby, don't get defensive. You're a fine half-blood and all. But there is no way you could possess the power to eliminate the entire vampire world. You couldn't even figure out Lucy was a killer and you decorate in all pink. No, no, I don't believe it for a moment."

My eyes narrowed but before I could call her out Piper asked Ileana a pointed question. "You know, I found vampire lore in *your* house, in *your* private library. Care to explain that?"

"Oh, all right." She sighed. "My father was a bit eccentric. He, well, he sort of worshipped vampires. Was obsessed with them actually. He found what he believed would be the Holy Grail to all vampires, this snippet of text." She sighed again, wearily. "All it got him was an Undead daughter and a shortened life span. Vampires, in my experience, are not a trustworthy lot."

I nodded in agreement, much to Thomas's annoyance.

"So that's why you had the lore? It was something your father found?"

"Yes, once I was changed I left my ancestral home and tried to keep a low profile. The vampire who created me didn't acquire a license so I didn't think he was going to tell anyone. Not that it mattered, he was killed shortly thereafter trying to raid another ancient's private library for more texts. I married the man I was betrothed to and he alone knew my secret. He loved me very much and we made plans. He sent me to one of his summer estates and vowed to join me later. That way I was kept in hiding and out of the way, as it were. Except, he died before he could join me. I stayed hidden and concocted the pregnancy plot. I knew I could eventually pass as my daughter."

"But you married several times after that," Piper couldn't help but interject.

"All fake marriages. I was a recluse and my husband left me a rich widow. I made up the weddings, the men, all of it. I even made up their deaths. Quite frankly, by the last husband I had run out of suitable accidents and resorted to an infected bug bite. But through it all I always had my maids." In a rare show of affection, Ileana patted Sophie on the arm, causing Sophie to blush to the roots of her hair.

"It's my honor, mum. I will serve as my mother served before me. It's my birthright," Sophie proclaimed with pride.

I felt sad for Ileana. Being practically alone all those years, hiding from the world to keep her secret safe, with no one but a maid for company. It was almost enough to forgive her prickly nature. Almost.

Piper seemed to rally and announced, "I almost forgot. I brought home presents." She ran upstairs and returned shortly with a brown shopping bag.

"Sorry, didn't have time to wrap them," she apologized as she started handing out what appeared to be T-shirts. I held up the one she gave me. It was white with pink lettering. On the front were our Greek letters and "Psi Phi" printed out over them. But the caption underneath held my attention. *We're not like the other girls.*

"What do you think?" Piper asked excitedly.

I looked at Thomas and declared, "I think they're perfect."

And now for a special preview from
Serena Robar's next exciting novel . . .

DATING FOR DEMONS

Available from Berkley!

found it hard to believe that such a big guy was even attempting to look inconspicuous while obviously following me, but there he was, *again*. This time he was feigning interest in some flamingo sunglasses while I cruised the Sunglass Hut. He was handsome in a bad boy, no, scratch that, in a *Piper* sort of way. I giggled at the thought. My best friend Piper Prescott would love the serious, dark vibe this guy was emitting. It would appeal to her whole, I'm-not-goth-I'm-alternative persona.

I took a deep breath once more and relaxed. He wasn't a vampire at least. Of that, I was sure. And he smelled like oatmeal raisin cookies with a hint of cinnamon. It was my experience (admittedly limited experience) that men who smelled like cookies were probably not evil. Yeah, it was pigeonholing an entire smell-type but hey, stereotypes existed for a reason, you know.

He may not be a vampire, but that didn't mean I shouldn't be cautious. It seemed every other night I was being attacked by some ancient vampire who followed The Prophesy, and occasionally they brought a human pet or two with them. They believed Colby Blanchard (that would be me) was the one who would bring the end to their existence. Tell a friend. Film at eleven. Sheesh, start a small revolution by emancipating half-blood vampires and suddenly, everyone thinks you're up to no good. It's not my fault that half-bloods were considered an abomination by all. But not anymore. I was a half-blood and proud of it. No one who dressed as well as I did was an abomination. Period.

No, this guy wasn't a vampire, and I thought it unlikely that he was a pet. Pets tended to be very robotic and couldn't think for themselves. They were under a vampire spell and looked spaced-out all the time. Nope, this guy could never be anyone's pet.

Maybe he was just shy and wanted to meet me? Probably. I mean, I looked pretty hot today with my spray-on tan and Psi Phi tank top. Sure it's the middle of April and still a bit chilly for the Northwest but when you're dead, er, Undead, a couple degrees didn't matter much. Call it a perk, if you will.

I made my way upstairs to the food court. I wanted Piper to meet me before the sun went down, but no, she was doing some homework and couldn't break away until the evening. As a half-blood, I was able to walk around during the day. Sure, I had to wear an SPF of about a gazillion, but I didn't mind.

I wasn't thrilled to meet Piper after dark though. What with all the kill-the-prophet-chick going on. I mean, putting your best friend in danger meant she wouldn't be your best friend for long. That was unacceptable. I needed Piper. I needed her like I needed sunlight, wait a minute, I didn't actually need sunlight and should really avoid it. Okay then, I needed her like I needed food. Hmm, I didn't need food either. Well, I needed Piper and I really shouldn't have to justify keeping my friends safe.

I reached the third floor and found her standing in line at Hot Dog on a Stick. I picked out a table and waited for her, shaking my head when I saw what she was wearing. Why, oh why did she have the fashion sense of a transient?

She sported Lucky Dungarees jeans with a white leather belt, ritually studded with metal brads in a uniform pattern. She'd paired a long-sleeved black mesh shirt, ripped at the collarbone and along one elbow, with a fitted burgundy tank over a black bra. Piper was short, around five four and curvy. That was to say she had a small waist, huge boobs and rounded bottom. She was wearing black Converse high-tops, natch. We wouldn't want to spread our wings and wear another pair of shoes or anything.

Still, with her shoulder-length jet-black hair, burgundy undertones and fondness for eyeliner, she had a style all her own. With her row of earrings and nose pierced, she was exotic, in a don't-sit-next-to-me-on-the-bus sort of way.

"Dew?" I inquired as she sipped some liquid through a straw. Piper lived off Mountain Dew.

"Nope, cherry lemonade."

I made a gagging sound in the back of my throat. Piper sure loved syrupy sweet drinks. And apparently, fried food on a stick. She'd bought a hot dog as well and it was smothered in mustard. I shuddered.

"Did you drag me all the way to the mall to insult my taste in beverages or did you have a real reason to meet here?"

She plopped down next to me, maneuvering her drink, plate and the monster size tote bag at her side.

"Bag lady," I muttered under my breath.

"I heard that," Piper said, not bothering to look up from her task of finding a portion of floor that was not sticky to deposit her tote.

"Do I need a reason to hang at the mall with my best friend?" I said brightly.

Piper was instantly suspicious. I guess I said it a little too brightly.

"What's wrong?"

"What do you mean 'What's wrong?'. Can't we get together outside the House for a little girl time at the mall without something being wrong?"

Piper just stared at me.

"Yeah, okay. Well, I was wondering if you'd made any progress on deciphering that stupid prophesy yet?" I hated to sound needy but I was kind of getting tired of being jumped every time I strolled around the park looking to find a little midnight snack.

"Were you attacked again?" Piper asked, concern replacing her normal sarcastic tone.

"Ah shucks, Piper. Are you worried about me?" I fluttered my eyelashes at her flirtatiously. Piper snorted.

"I know how to stop the attacks," she said deadpan, her face filled with earnest.

"Really?" I said, leaning forward, excited she'd finally uncovered the truth about the prophesy. "How?"

"Quit dressing like a streetwalker."

I blinked once. Twice. Not sure if I heard her correctly. She laughed at my expression, no longer able to hold a straight face.

"Oh, hardy-har-har," my voice dripped acid.

"Don't you think if I'd found the true meaning of the prophesy, I would have called you right away?" she questioned after her laughter died down.

"Yeah, I'm just getting tired of playing dodge the stake, and last night, well"—I shook my head in remembrance—"I was dodging a sword. A freakin' *sword*, Piper. I mean who walks around campus waving a sword and doesn't get busted by campus security?"

Piper sat up straighter and demanded, "Did you tell Thomas?"

I nibbled on my lower lip wondering how to answer that one. "I would have told Thomas," I ventured slowly, "but he has a lot going on right now with all the rogue vampires attacking people and stuff."

Thomas was my Vampire Investigator boyfriend and a fullblood. He'd helped me when I was first changed and we'd grown pretty close in the last year. Yet lately, well, I didn't want to burden Piper about Thomas's weird loner behavior lately. I mean, he was working his cute butt off nightly trying to keep the public safe from vampires who were freaking out about some stupid prophesy that thought I was going to destroy their existence. Puh-lease, like I would if I could.

"It's Thomas's job to protect the people and get the bad vampires. He can handle it. He would want to know, Colby."

She was right, of course. He would want to know, but I really didn't want to add to his workload. He was even having nightmares when he slept and they were really unnerving. I didn't even like to cuddle next to him when he slept anymore because they bothered me so much, and once, well, once he'd swung out as though he were fighting some unknown foe and knocked me right out of the bed. When I woke him he didn't remember a thing. He claimed he wasn't having them anymore, but the dark circles under his eyes told me another story. He wanted to protect me as much as I wanted to protect him. Boy, did we have control issues or what?

"Yeah, I know. I plan to tell him, I just hoped I could add good news with the bad, like, I was attacked with a sword last night but Piper figured out the prophesy so hey, there won't be anymore pin-the-sword-through-the-Colby night games."

"Sorry to disappoint," Piper said rolling her corn dog around in the mustard, trying to gob on even more, if that was even possible.

"You're gonna get a stomachache," I warned as she took a bite.

"You're just jealous because I can eat real food," she gloated.

"You know a real friend wouldn't rub that in and probably wouldn't even eat in front of me," I pouted prettily.

She took another bite and chewed with her mouth open, showing me everything I was missing.

"Ew, gross!"

She smacked her lips after swallowing and smiled smugly.

"Fine, next time I'm hungry, I'll feed in front of you." It was an empty threat. I wasn't about to let Piper watch me suck down a pint of O negative from some unsuspecting victim. Piper had a very weak stomach.

Ignoring me, she asked, "How is Aunt Chloe doing as your housemother?"

I rolled my eyes in answer. Aunt Chloe was actually my great, great aunt but everyone just called her Aunt Chloe. She used to be a nurse during WWII and the Korean War. She was feisty and opinionated and was currently acting as Psi Phi House sorority mother.

"It's only temporary. A big façade actually. I can't believe the administration threatened to revoke our sorority status because we didn't have a live-in housemother. Sheesh. I'm glad Aunt Chloe is helping us out but I think she misses her friends at Providence Point and candidly, she is getting downright bossy."

Aunt Chloe normally lived in an upper-scale retirement community on the Eastside, but when I needed a housemother ASAP, she packed her bags and moved in. All without my consent, might I add. In theory, it was a good fit. She knew I was Undead and knew that all the girls at Psi Phi House were half-bloods as well. She wasn't even squeamish about sleeping in the same room where we found a murdered half-blood hidden in a trunk last year.

"Pish posh," she'd said when I objected to her sleeping in that room. "There isn't a day gone by I don't see an ambulance picking up a body somewhere in Providence Point. People die, Colby. That's part of the cycle. Nothing to be scared of." And that was basically Aunt Chloe in a nutshell. She was one tough, ol' bird.

"Bossy? How?" Piper wanted to know.

"Well, first of all she gave us all household chores and harps on us constantly to get them done. She even made us a chart! She decided it was much too important to trust us to make our own study times so she instituted set Quiet Time study sessions where attendance is mandatory. She claims the girls lack discipline and need to understand the importance of passing their Undead courses. Seems to me everyone understands if they don't pass the course, they don't get a vampire license and without that, they are relieved of their Undead status. You know." I made swift cutting motion across my neck to emphasize my point. "They all get how important the classes are to their existence."

"Sounds like she is just trying to help," Piper noted.

"Tell that to Sage. She put her on a diet."

Piper looked shocked. "How do you put a vampire on a diet? And for that matter, why put her on a diet? You guys stay the same after you die, right?"

"Only full-bloods apparently. Sage, for some weird reason, is able to consume milk products. And she loves shakes. Has them all the time. She is forever walking to Starbucks and getting a frapuccino after her nightly feeding. Anyway, we all noticed she had to go out and buy new clothes, 'cause her other ones were too tight. Her face was getting rounder and finally Aunt Chloe tells her she is getting fat. I mean right to her face she says, 'Sage, you're getting fat. I'm putting you on a diet.'"

Piper made a noise somewhere between a gasp of dismay and a chortle of laughter.

"I know," I agreed with the sentiment behind the sound, "I couldn't believe it either. Sage got all flustered and embarrassed but Aunt Chloe didn't relent. She made Sage a chart as well, to keep count of her daily shake intake."

"That's awful."

I shrugged. "I'd rather be on the diet chart than the boy chart."

"I'm almost afraid to ask what the boy chart is," Piper said.

I smirked at her. "Remember last fall when our football team was being affected by a strange illness that was making them all weak and lightheaded?"

Piper shook her head. "Vaguely."

"It seemed the basketball team was struck with the same mysterious illness. The guys were passing out in practice and no one, not the coaches or the team doctors could figure out why. But Aunt Chloe did."

"How?"

"She hears things right? She listens to the girls talking about their nightly feedings and who is dating who and then announces the boy chart one night. She tells us each time we feed from an athlete, we put their name under our column and no one can feed on the same athlete for at least two weeks. It appeared that several of the girls have a thing for jocks and each of them were hooking up and feeding on the same guys. These guys were literally being sucked dry by Psi Phi House."

Piper let out a bark of laughter, then clamped a hand over her mouth when everyone in the food court turned to stare. She shook with the effort to hold it in, but couldn't seem to stop giggling.

"Sure, laugh it up. It was pretty shocking for the girls to see their favorite flavor on another girl's column. I thought Angie was going to stake one of the new girls, Manda, after seeing three of her favorite treats under her name."

"Are you on the ho chart?" Piper asked suddenly.

"It's called the boy chart," I corrected primly. "And no, I am not. I have Thomas and I never feed on the same person twice."

I didn't elaborate on the fact that Thomas had such rich blood that I could feed on him and not need to eat for the rest of the day, and vice versa. Anyway, feeding with Thomas was not like feeding on a stranger. It had an entirely different effect on me and I wasn't about to share that with Piper.

"Yeah, I bet." She smirked at me, but I didn't rise to the bait.

"So, back to the prophesy. How's progress?" I felt it was prudent to change the subject or Piper would figure out feeding was a passionate pastime between Thomas and myself. I was relieved when she let it go.

"Actually, I have some leads that sound promising. I need you to take me to the vampire library. I heard they have several ancient scripts in the back."

"They are never going to let you in the library, much less nose around in the private collections," I told her.

"Is it because of the whole 'I breathe therefore I live thing'?" Piper quipped

"Something like that. Tell me what to look for and I'll try to see them."

"Try? You mean you don't know if you can look at the private stuff either?"

"The librarian and I don't really see eye to eye." I reluctantly admitted. "I don't think she likes me."

"Imagine that." Piper said dryly. "A full-blood who doesn't like the half-blood Protector. Shocker."

I nodded. "Hard to believe that I'm not loved and adored by the entire full-blood population, but there you go. I'll see if Mr. Holloway can get me access."

Mr. Holloway was a member of the Vampire Tribunal. He was one of the three head-honcho vampires and I kind of keep a dark secret of his, so he's willing to do stuff for me.

"Failing that, I guess we pay a little visit during the day."

"You mean break in?" Piper clarified.

"Geez, when you put it like that is sounds so sordid, Piper," I complained and she laughed at me.

"Fine, but I get to be Bonnie. You're Clyde," she teased, referring to a couple of famous old-time bad guys.

"I was thinking more along the lines of Charlie's Angels, but whatever."

We were silent a moment when I noticed Piper looking over my shoulder, her mouth forming a small O of surprise. It didn't take a rocket scientist to figure out my stalker had stepped out of the shadows. And I was so right, he was definitely Piper's type, if the look on her face was any indication.